DUSTY AYRES AND HIS BATTLE BIRDS:
THE TESLA RAIDERS

THE TESLA RAIDERS

By Robert Sidney Bowen

ALTUS PRESS • 2019

EDITED AND DESIGNED BY

Matthew Moring

PUBLISHING HISTORY

"The Tesla Raiders" originally appeared in the July–August, 1935 (Vol. 8, No. 3) issue
of *Dusty Ayres and his Battle Birds* magazine. Copyright 2019 by Steeger Properties,
LLC. All rights reserved.

CHAPTER 1
SECRET ORDERS

NIGHT, SILENT and sombre, shrouded the small field in a blanket of inky darkness. A thin cloud layer blotted out the stars, and even the glow of a full moon was diffused into nothingness before it could reach earth.

On one side of the field were two buildings. One small, and one large, and both obviously hastily constructed. In the larger one a faint light showed behind the drawn blinds of a window. At fifty yards, it would not have been noticed. But it was there, nevertheless.

Inside the room, seated about a massive table were six men in the uniform of the Black Invaders. Insignia differed, but the uniforms in general were the same. At one end of the table there was an empty chair. It was a big chair, almost big enough for any two in that room to sit in together, comfortably.

Like the night outside, the room inside was devoid of any sound. For all the noise there was, the six figures could have been six dead men. True, they moved every now and then. One of them would turn to stare at the big chair, crease his heavy brows in puzzled, perhaps worried thought, and then return his gaze to the table top littered with papers. And, like it was some sort of a game, another one of them would go through the silent procedure.

Strangely enough, though, they never looked at one another.

The Telsa Raiders

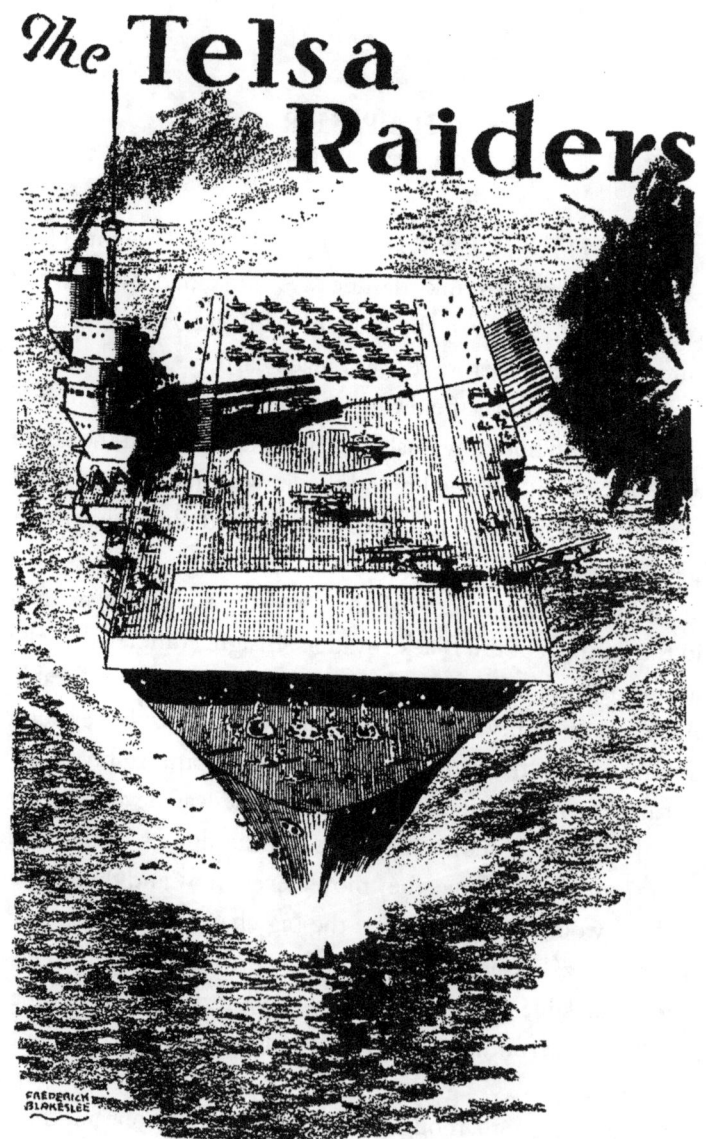

FREDERICK
BLAKESLEE

by ROBERT SIDNEY BOWEN

As a matter of fact, it was quite evident that they steadfastly avoided it. When eyes locked by accident, each pair immediately was cast elsewhere, usually to study intently the papers on the desk.

There was nothing but silence, yet so strained and tensed that a hidden observer would have instinctively steeled himself for an explosion.

Outside the building, moving slowly up and down the rim of the field made soft and mushy by the rains and thaw of late Spring, were five Black Invader soldiers. Like the officers inside the room, they too were silent.

In the manner of guardians of the dead, they moved back and forth, back and forth, passing and repassing one another. But not once did so much as a grunt come from their lips. Unlike the officers in the room, however, they cast furtive, searching glances at each other. It was as though each soldier tried to fathom the thoughts of the next man from the expression on his face.

Midnight slid by into history. The cloud layer thickened, and even the diffused light of the moon was no longer visible. A cold wind from the Atlantic swept across the southern tip of Nova Scotia, where the field was located, and chilled the bones of those soldiers moving back and forth. They tugged their great-coats tighter about them, and kept on with their seemingly endless and nonsensical routine.

Another hour dragged by. And then, from out of the eastern heavens came the soft swishing sound of man-made wings sweeping down. As one man, the five soldiers stopped short, stiffened to the alert and took a firmer grip on their rifles.

Louder and louder grew the sound. And presently a darker, moving blur was visible against the inky background. With eerie majesty it swooped lower and lower, until it seemed almost to brush the tips of trees bordering the eastern end of the field.

A moment later a white light arced out and down and the moving blur touched the ground. Wheels were rolling slowly over the mushy soil, and above the wheels was a giant monoplane wing and a barrel-shaped, round-nosed cabin fuselage.

As the plane moved toward the larger of the two buildings, the one in which the light showed behind drawn blinds, the soldiers moved with it. And when it stopped, they stopped also—four statues of immovable flesh and bones, the biting wind off the Atlantic notwithstanding.

With a weird sigh, like that of a tired animal, the propellers stopped turning, became horizontal and motionless. A door on the right side of the fuselage opened, and in the faint glow cast back by an instrument board cowl lamp, the figure of a Black Invader officer jumped down to the ground, turned back toward the door at rigid attention.

Then the glow of the cowl lamp was blotted out by a massive hulk in the cabin doorway. The hulk stepped down, straightened up and immediately dwarfed the officer at attention. Like the roll of thunder in the distance, the sound came from the massive hulk; a voice was speaking in the curious jargon of the Black Invaders.

"Wait in your plane. Do not leave it for an instant. I will give you further orders later!"

The officer snapped up his right hand, shoulder-high and palm outward, in the salute of the Invaders, and stepped back smartly one pace. The giant of a man strode over to the door of the large building, thrust it open and stepped into the lighted room. The six officers in that room were already on their feet, already at rigid salute. And as the towering hulk entered, the same cry of homage burst from every throat.

"*He-e-e la-a-a zo!*"

The cry bounced around the walls, died out sharply as the big figure at the opened door raised a black-gauntleted hand. Still rigid, the six officers silently watched the big figure move toward the empty chair at the end of the table. They looked at his loose-fitting Black uniform of coarse material, at the single insignia he wore; a length of green-gold braid on each shoulder-strap.

They looked at the three-quarter length black gauntlets that covered his hands, and the tight-fitting black skull-cap that came down over the nape of his neck.

They looked at the three-quarter-length mask that completely covered his face. But most of all, they looked at the two eye-slits in that mask; at the orbs of fire glittering through the slits.

HE, WHO owned their very lives, and did with them as he wished, was in their midst. He who had flung his bloody challenge to the entire world, and had already crushed half of it under his iron heel, was towering over them. He, Fire-Eyes, self-styled Emperor of the World, and supreme commander of the civilization-destroying Black Invaders, had arrived in the western hemisphere, direct from his European stronghold.

Slowly the Black commander sank into the chair. For a few seconds those horrible blazing eyes swept every face before them. Then the man gestured, and the six officers sat down stiffly, waited. They did not have to wait long. The voice from behind the mask boomed out like the clap of doomsday.

"I return to you for explanations. None of you has accomplished anything of merit during my absence. On land, on water and in the air you have acted like fools. I pardon mistakes, but I do not pardon fools. You were told what must be accomplished while I was away. You had the men and you had the equipment but you allowed these dog Americans, and a handful of Canadians to make fools of you. You lost instead of winning! You retreated instead of going forward! I return for explanations. Let them be short and to the point! And let them be satisfactory, for your sakes!"

The Black commander chopped off his words, turned his blazing eyes on the officer to his left.

"You will speak first!" he thundered. "Two army corps, guns and ammunition enough for all, and you have not advanced a single foot. Speak!"

The officer stood up, and the infantry insignia on his uniform sparkled in the light of the single bulb overhead.

"The weather, Supreme One!" he said. "The Americans withdrew to strong positions. It would have been but throwing away gallant troops for a few miles of snow and ice-buried waste. Instead, I prepared and schooled them for a successful onslaught when you, Supreme One, should give the word of command."

The blazing orbs moved on the next officer.

"And you?"

"The same, Supreme One. I remembered the lesson I learned during the conquest of the Soviet. But now we are prepared to sweep down and take the entire Chicago area, and more, with small losses."

Fire-Eyes directed his terrible gaze on the third officer, and the fourth. Both wore the uniform of high-ranking Black Navy officers.

"Let one speak for both!" the command boomed out. "Let

one of you explain why these American rowboats are so formidable against our men-of-war!"

The second of the pair rose to his feet, swallowed hard and threw back his shoulders.

"They are ours for the taking, Supreme One—if they will but put to sea and give battle. But the Supreme One has given us his orders—we are to avoid contact with American coast defense forces. Since the Supreme One has been away, the American fleets have steamed close to their shores. They have come out into deep waters for short periodic raids only—raids which we have beaten back successfully."

"Successfully?" came the booming echo. "Twenty of our finest ships at the bottom of the Atlantic and the Pacific? Your teeth have lost their sharpness. The United States navy has played with you as it saw fit. Both of you will speak again with me, later."

The blood drained from the faces of the two naval officers, leaving them as masks of wax out of which burned haunted eyes—haunted eyes dully glazed with the fear of expected death. But what might happen later did not matter. Those two were already dead. The actual stopping of their hearts would be only a formality. The one standing wilted down into his chair, and both slumped forward against the edge of the table.

In the meantime, the burning orbs behind the slitted green mask swept around the table to the fifth officer.

"And you? Have your eyes stopped seeing? And have your ears stopped hearing? American Intelligence has been accomplishing its tasks right under your nose. Its leader, that dog

General Horner, has placed his cursed agents everywhere—placed them in our very ranks, while you have been asleep. And what have your agents found out for you—nothing that we did not already know. Speak up! Must I make a change in my Intelligence service as there will be made in my navy?"

The fifth officer got to his feet. Though his lean, cruel-featured face was a trifle pale, his eyes were steady and brittle. They stared unflinchingly into the slitted green mask.

"Supreme One," came the steady voice, "my report is to be given to you when we are alone. I trust no one's ears but your own. That request I now make—and I place my life as the forfeit should the granting of it not prove completely satisfactory to the Supreme One."

Tingling silence settled over the room for almost thirty seconds. The green mask moved slowly from side to side, and all six officers seated at that table were held in the grip of those terrible blazing orbs. Then suddenly the Black commander nodded.

"Very well, the request is granted. You still seem to show signs of possessing brains. Let us hope that you will not be required to pay the forfeit."

"Thank you, Supreme One," said the other, and he reseated himself.

The sixth and last officer of the group was now the focal point of the Black commander. And when the voice boomed out again, it did something that it had not done with the other five. It spoke in a slightly reproachful tone—and it pronounced a name.

"And you, Zytoff? The one upon whom I counted so much. The only one whom I believed would not fail me. To you was entrusted the most important task of all. And it collapsed in the space of two days. Weeks, months of diligent preparation—swept away from us in two short days. What have you to say?"

Slowly, Zytoff, most favored of all Fire-Eyes' aides, stood up. He was taller than any of the other five. And he was far better looking, too. Save for the uniform he wore, he could be taken for an American, or a Canadian. In fact, he had all the appearance of an All-American half-back—he was built that way.

But apart from his looks, he of all the others showed not the single trace of fear as he looked at his senior officer. Not one drop of blood faded from his well-featured face. And not a single tremor of dubious misapprehension crept into his voice as he spoke—spoke with the self-assurance of an educated and cultured man.

"My failure, Supreme One," he said, "is my fault, and mine alone. I blame no one but myself. And I blame myself for over-eagerness to serve you doubly. I struck too soon. Had our secret base in the American Rocky Mountains been more firmly established before I struck, it is quite probable that failure in my first venture on this side of the Atlantic would not have been my lot."

The man paused, waited for Fire-Eyes to speak. The Black commander hesitated but a few seconds.

"WERE IT not for European successes, Zytoff, you would now be a doomed man. That, and the fact I have need of your services on another project. But first—how do you explain your failure? Six weeks ago, you were safely hidden in the very heart of the United States. Hidden deep in the Rocky Mountains— in a perfect position to deal smashing blows at this upstart nation that has dared to defy us. And now—everything lost; time, energy, expense wasted!"

ZYTOFF

For the first time, Zytoff showed signs of emotion. His jaw muscles tightened, and he bit deeply into his lower lip.

"Two men," he said suddenly. "Two American dogs—well known to even the Supreme One. They are Captain Ayres and his flying comrade, Lieutenant Brooks. I confess that I had them both as my prisoners. And then—"

Zytoff shrugged, half gestured.

"And then I had them as prisoners no longer. And I was fighting for my own life. I can but say, it shall never happen again. It was our first meeting, and I curse myself for underestimating their ability."

Fire-Eyes heard him through to the end. Then he raised one clenched fist and smashed it down on the table. The papers fluttered about like dried leaves. Some of them slid off onto the floor, to lay there unnoticed and untouched.

"Captain Ayres!" the Black commander thundered. "Must I always be hearing his thrice-cursed name as an excuse for failure by my commanders. Are you all rabbits—afraid of him? Is he not but one man, with but one heart to be stopped? Most certainly he is. He is not an army—just one man! And you let him walk out of your traps and thwart you at every turn.

"Well, you have let him do so for the last time. If Captain Ayres is ever captured alive again, and he escapes alive—the man responsible will die without any form of trial. That is so with you army and navy commanders, as it is with Zytoff of my air force. Do you all understand?"

Six heads bobbed up and down, like six puppets of a Punch and Judy show. Their commander swept them with his blazing eyes, then reached a gauntleted hand under the side flap of his tunic and drew forth six sealed envelopes. He spread them out like cards between the gloved fingers of his hand, and held them up for all to see.

"I shall give you men of my navy one more chance," Fire-Eyes boomed, pointing to the two cringing admirals, "but if you fail me this time you will wish that you had never been born!

"Here is a copy of my secret orders for each of you! Only as they affect your own particular branch of my forces do they differ. In over a year we have only succeeded in capturing a paltry few hundred square miles of American territory.

"I am through with being patient. I am through listening to the counsel of those who did such splendid work in Europe and in Asia. The United States of America is our main enemy now. I intended to crush it once and for all. We will—"

There was a sharp knock at the door. The green mask did not move, but the blazing eyes behind the slits leaped toward it.

"Enter!"

The door swung open to reveal two figures in the uniform of the Black Invaders. One figure, however, dragged the other into the room, and as he hurled him down onto the floor, blood spattered from an ugly gash down the left side of the fallen man's face. The other turned to Fire-Eyes, saluted.

"You may speak!" boomed the Black commander.

"He is a dog American agent, Supreme One," pointing to the limp figure on the floor. "I surprised him in the radio room. He was contacting his headquarters."

Fire-Eyes interrupted him with a bellow that made even the walls of the room tremble.

"And what was the message? Speak! Have you no longer a tongue in your head?"

The newcomer shrank back from those horrible eyes, ran a dry tongue over an even drier lower lip.

"Speak, fool! What was the message he was sending?"

"That, I do not know, Supreme One," came the quavering reply. "He stopped as I entered—tried to fire a gas gun he had. But I was too quick for him. My knife struck into his face, and he fell before he could pull the trigger."

"Then how do you know he is an American agent?" the other roared. "How do you know he was contacting American head-quarters? Did you just guess all this?"

The shrinking man shook his head so hard that his teeth rattled, and his eyeballs popped in their sockets.

"The message recorder, Supreme One!" he implored, as though he expected Fire-Eyes to smash him to the floor before he could get the words out. "It was registered on the official American headquarters wave-length signal. He had been signaling to them for three minutes. That I noticed, too. And he tried to kill me!"

The man would have continued babbling on, but Fire-Eyes silenced him with a gesture of his gauntleted hand.

"You have seen him before? Seen him here at this place?"

"Yes, Supreme One. I have seen him for the last week, but not before that!"

A LOW grunt came from behind the green mask, and Fire-Eyes slowly turned toward the head of his Intelligence service. The Intelligence chief's face went deathly white, and he stared at the Black commander like a hypnotized bird stares at a snake. Then the thundering voice smote him with the fury of a tornado.

"A week he has been here! One week ago I sent secret word of when I would arrive. The dog Americans knew—and one of them has been waiting here. Waiting right under your nose, you blundering, blind fool!"

The Intelligence chief's lips opened, but no sound came from between them. Fire-Eyes suddenly ignored him, rose from his chair and walked around the table to the figure on the floor.

"Pull him to his feet!" he boomed. "Let me have a look at him."

The latest arrival bent over, jerked his charge cruelly up onto his feet. The whole left side of the man's face was now a sticky mass of fresh blood. The other side was chalk-white in direct contrast. Dulled eyes slowly came up, riveted on the green mask.

"Better make it good, big shot! There's not much more time to play soldier!"

The words, rasping with pain, came off the wounded man's lips in defiant tone. Fire-Eyes reached out a gloved hand, curled his fingers in the loose front of the man's tunic, and held him at arm's length so that only the toes of his boots touched the floor. Thin, pale, pain-twisted lips somehow went back in a grin.

"Can you play 'the little pig goes to market,' too?"

Fire-Eyes twisted his clenched hand and the man gasped with pain.

"You sent word of my arrival, American dog?" the Black commander bellowed. "You sent word through to your dog superior, General Horner?"

The answer came in a weak, wheezing whisper.

"What do you think, dearie?"

Fire-Eyes started to twist again, but for some reason checked himself.

"You will answer my question!" he boomed. "Or you will be through with life forever! What was the message that you sent through to your Washington headquarters? Answer me, instantly!"

The unknown Yank agent made horrible gurgling sound as he sucked in his breath.

"Okay, I'll tell you," he managed to get out. "I forgot an extra suit of underwear when I left. So I asked a pal to send it along to—"

The man went spinning back, crashed up against the far wall. Blood spattered from the ugly gash on his face. Eyes closed, body completely limp, he slid down onto the floor and lay still.

Fire-Eyes pointed a finger.

"Take him away, and shoot straight!" he thundered. "One shot will be enough."

Without waiting for the newcomer to salute, the Black commander walked back to his chair, sat down and picked up the six envelopes. When the door closed behind the Yank agent and his appointed executioner, Fire-Eyes spoke again.

"That they know of my return does not change my plans," he began. "Fortunately I foresaw that possibility, and accordingly, made arrangements. But as I was saying, here are my secret orders. If they are carried out to the letter—no slips, and no mistakes—the American nation will be ours!"

Fire-Eyes leaned over the table, tapped the sealed envelopes with the forefinger of his other gloved hand.

"One cuts the loaf of bread into slices before he eats it," he said suddenly. "America is our loaf of bread, and so we shall cut it into slices. First, one slice, then a second slice. And after that—"

The Black commander extended his free hand, slowly curled the fingers until they formed a massive hammerhead fist. Instantly the six others leaped to their feet, and the roaring cry resounded about the room.

"He-e-e la-a-a zo!"

CHAPTER 2
"KIDNAP FIRE-EYES!"

IN A long graceful glide, Dusty Ayres slid his X-Diesel down onto the Washington military field, touched rubber and taxied quickly into the hangar line.

Legging out he nodded at a couple of greaseballs, old friends of his, who ran out to take charge of his ship, and then turned curious eyes toward the figure of Jack Horner walking rapidly toward him.

When the Intelligence ace reached him and they exchanged mutual greetings, Dusty put the question that had been uppermost in his mind all the way from the home drome of High Speed Group No. 7.

"What's it all about this time, kid? I smoked down here right after your message same through. Haven't decided to pay me that drink you owe me, have you?"

Jack Horner, known to a selected few as Agent 10, grinned, took hold of Dusty's arm, and steered him over toward a parked staff car.

"I'd buy you that drink," he said, "when you buy me the half dozen you owe me. But seriously, how's the studying coming along? Have you got the hang of the rising inflection at the end of each sentence?"

Dusty grunted a curse.

"I'll say I have, and so will Curly! Boy, can I rip off Black Invader lingo now—and how! Curly threatens to shoot me if I don't do my practicing in the woods. He vows I've spoiled his last night of sleep.

"Funny, I thought the stuff would be hard to catch onto. Matter of fact though, it came easy. At least, so far. But, what's up? Am I to be given a language examination?"

"Maybe," replied Agent 10 as they reached the car. "Get in. No, on the other side. I want to keep my blood pressure down, so I'll drive."

Dusty shrugged, went around to the other side and climbed in. Eyes puzzled, he watched his friend get behind the wheel and start the car rolling forward.

He hadn't seen young Horner for almost three weeks. At that time the Intelligence ace had visited him at his home drome, dumped a bunch of Black Invader language books in his lap, and told him to go to it and master what he could of the lingo.

He'd taken it with a grin, but to his surprise he discovered the next day that Major Drake had grounded him—practically forbidden him to fly beyond the confines of the field, and ordered him to comply with Jack Horner's request.

Questioning the major hadn't gained Dusty a single thing.

The C.O. himself didn't know the answer. And he admitted that his orders for Dusty to learn as much as he could of the Black Invader language, had come through direct from General Bradley, chief of the U.S. air force.

DUSTY AYRES

The result was that he'd studied—studied day and night, much to the annoyance of Curly Brooks and Biff Bolton. It had been hard work, but interesting, and Dusty had made rapid progress. Then, today, word had come from young Horner for him to fly at once to the Washington military field.

And now, here he was, bursting with questions, and getting one riddle after another for answers. He smothered a curse, fished out a cigarette and lighted up.

"Charming weather you're having down here in Washington," he greeted. "Or hadn't you noticed?"

Jack Horner grinned with one side of his mouth.

"It has been nice, up until today," he said. "Looks, though, like its clouding up for a storm. However, I've weathered storms before. And how are all your folks, captain?"

"Nuts, lieutenant!" Dusty snapped, sliding down lower in the seat. "Keep your blasted answers, and the hell with you!"

"*Tsk, tsk!*" And I've been looking forward to seeing you again. Ah, well! But if it helps your feelings any—I don't know the answers myself! I'm in the dark, the same as you."

Dusty sat up.

"Huh?"

"I said, I was in the dark the same as you. Getting you to study the lingo, and getting you down here today, all came from the general, not me. The father wouldn't even tell his own son, see? So, call off your dogs. Get sore at General Horner, if you must. But lay off Lieutenant Horner."

Dusty stared thoughtfully ahead at the road for several minutes.

"I once knew a Lieutenant Horner," he murmured, "who didn't have to be told very much. He was one swell guesser, if you know what I mean. Damnedest guy for reading between the lines you ever saw."

"Knew him quite well myself," grinned the Intelligence ace. "But I hear he's been slipping plenty of late. Can't hardly guess the time of day."

"Let it pass," Dusty grumbled. "Couldn't get it out of you

even if I used a gun. But now I know what Curly and Biff must think of me sometimes."

As Dusty stopped, they both lapsed into a silence that continued until Agent 10 braked the car to a full stop at the curb edge in front of the towering war department building.

The Intelligence man taking the lead, they climbed out, went up the long flight of wide stone steps, in through the big doors, and along the tiled lobby to the first of the row of express elevators.

A nod from Agent 10, and the operator, in staff-private uniform, whizzed them aloft to the fifty-seventh floor. Still leading the two-man parade, young Horner went past a desk, where sat a bristling-mustached major who gave them a cold quizzical look, and on down the corridor to the end where it branched off to the right.

Halfway down the branch corridor he stopped in front of a door and knocked. It was opened immediately, and a steel-eyed guard stuck his head out. Then he immediately jerked it back and swung the door open for them to pass through.

The door led into a small outer office that Dusty recognized at once. As a matter of fact, he'd had a pretty good idea where they were headed when they'd stepped off the elevator. And coming into this small office proved him correct. On the door on the other side were the printed words:

General J.T. Horner
PRIVATE

"Go right ahead, sir. The general is expecting you."

Agent 10 nodded his thanks to the guard, gave Dusty the eye and crossed the room to the other door. Instead of knocking, he jabbed a thumb button on the right side of the jamb.

A few seconds clicked past, and then the door was opened and the big form of General Horner, chief of Intelligence, confronted them. He swept them both with a single glance, stepped to one side and motioned them through. Slamming the door behind them he turned; and smiling at Dusty, put out his hand.

"Glad to see you, Ayres," he rumbled in his deep voice. "You're looking fit."

Dusty accepted the hand, shook it warmly.

"Thank you, sir," he said. "And I guess I can say the same about you, too, sir."

THE PILOT'S lips lied, and none knew it better than he. General Horner was a long way from looking fit. To be truthful, he looked like a man about ready to cave in and collapse completely.

Every line in his face was a line left by worry and uneasiness. Only his steel-gray eyes, piercing out from beneath shaggy eyebrows, were of normal appearance. And even they held a veiled light of strained inner emotions.

The senior officer's voice, however, was calm and steady. So were his movements, as he walked around in back of a big desk, and pointed at a couple of chairs.

"Be seated, gentlemen," he said. "You'll find cigarettes in the ivory box, there, on the corner. Smoke if you wish."

Dusty took advantage of the hesitant silence that followed

by lighting up and holding the match for Jack Horner. Then spewing smoke ceilingward, he settled back and fastened his eyes on the general.

"You've been studying the Black Invader language, Ayres?"

The question came suddenly, and unexpectedly. Dusty nodded his head.

"Yes sir," he said. "I've learned quite a bit of it, too. But of course, it's only been three weeks."

The senior officer bobbed his head up and down.

"Yes, only three weeks," he muttered absently. "Too bad it isn't longer. Well, can't be helped, I'm afraid."

The man's voice trailed off. He half turned and sat staring out the window—as though he was watching something taking place far, far away. Unconsciously, Dusty turned his head, and looked out the window, too.

He saw a broad expanse of light blue, dotted here and there with a few clouds, their fleecy edges tinged a deep crimson by the rays of a setting sun. When he turned back, it was to discover that General Horner's gaze was now fixed upon him intently.

"It's a funny question, Ayres," the words shot out quickly, "but what would you be willing to sacrifice to defeat the purposes of the Black Invaders?"

Dusty sat up, frowned, and snubbed out his cigarette in the ashtray on the desk.

"Anything and everything, sir," he replied quietly. "And I think you know that."

"I do. Call it a quirk of the brain, but I wanted to hear it from your own lips. Well—I'm speaking to both of you now—I'm going to offer you the opportunity to do, perhaps, that very thing. I mean, sacrifice everything—even your lives."

Neither Dusty nor young Horner moved a single muscle. Human statues, they sat there waiting for the other to continue speaking. But Dusty, at least, was momentarily disappointed. The general reached out his hand toward the inter-department call-set on his desk.

"Excuse me a second," he said, and flipped up a switch and jabbed a button.

Then he bent toward the built-in speaker unit.

"General Horner's compliments!" he snapped. "Ask General Bradley to step over here right away."

A voice said, "Very good, sir," and the general snapped off contact.

For the next two or three minutes Dusty had nothing to do but twiddle his thumbs. Shooting questioning looks at the general was most unproductive. The senior officer was busily occupied with some papers on his desk. And when Dusty looked at Agent 10, the Intelligence ace simply hunched his shoulders and arched his eyebrows.

Finally, though, a desk buzzer broke the silence. General Horner looked at his son and nodded. Young Horner went over to the door, opened it and ushered General Bradley, chief of the air force staff, into the room. Everyone exchanged greetings, and presently all were seated about the desk.

"I haven't told Captain Ayres a thing yet, Bradley," General

Horner said to the air force head. "Out of courtesy to your department, I want you to say anything you wish first."

"Thank you, Horner," smiled the other. "I'll leave the details to you though."

Then turning to Dusty.

"However, Ayres," he said, "as your chief, I want you to understand that any decision you make regarding what General Horner has to say will be entirely up to you, and up to you alone.

"Whether you accept, or refuse, will have no bearing whatsoever upon your standing in the air force, or upon my own personal feelings toward you. It is a decision which I shall neither ask nor order you to make—either way. You understand perfectly?"

Dusty grinned.

"I guess so, sir," he said. "I'll know better when I hear what it's all about."

General Bradley looked at General Horner, and the Intelligence chief looked at Dusty, cleared his throat in a nervous gesture.

"We have it on absolute authority, Ayres," he shot out, "that Fire-Eyes has returned to Black territory in Canada!"

DUSTY TOOK it calmly. Like thousands of others who knew that the Black commander had gone back to Europe, he didn't expect the mystery man of war to stay there for the rest of his life. He nodded slightly and spoke because he felt that General Horner expected him to say something.

"Back, eh, sir? Then I guess we can prepare for trouble. When did he return?"

"Last night," was the reply. "We've been expecting him for the last week. One of my men got word through to me—at least enough for me to understand. Something happened before he completed the whole message."

Dusty glanced at Agent 10, saw his jaw muscles tighten and his eyes go agate. He could read what was in his friend's mind as though it were an open book. Swiveling his eyes back to the Intelligence head, he nodded again.

"Did he say what we could expect, sir?" he asked.

The other didn't answer directly. Picking up a pencil, he drummed it softly on the desk, furrowed his brows in heavy thought.

"No," he rumbled suddenly. "That's the part we didn't get—assuming, of course, that he did know. And I doubt that very much."

Before Dusty could say anything, he continued on.

"For once, Fire-Eyes has sewn up his secrets tighter than a drum! Reports from our contacts in Europe have given us no news at all. That is, no news that we can act upon.

"It is well known that Fire-Eyes intends to strike harder than ever; well known that he has been preparing all Winter and all Spring to strike that blow—or blows. But when, where, and how, are three questions we haven't been able to answer. Rumors and wild guesses, yes! Hundreds of them! Thousands! But nothing concrete. Not a damn thing!"

The Intelligence chief lapsed into silence, moodily studied an imaginary pattern he traced on the desk with the end of his pencil. Dusty did his best to control his curiosity and his rising annoyance.

General Horner and his son were two of the finest men God ever created, but they drove him plumb frantic at times. Perhaps it was the result of their Intelligence training and experience. But at any rate, it was like pulling teeth to get them to the crux of anything secret and important. And even then he had to drag the words out of them.

He stood the silence as long as he could, leaned forward and rested his hands on the desk.

"Perhaps he's getting underway right now, sir," he said meaningly. "What's the plan in the back of your mind?"

General Horner smiled rather faintly.

"You'd make a poor army commander, Ayres, with your perpetual eagerness for direct action," he said. "Then, again, perhaps you'd prove to be the perfect leader. It's hard to say. However, that's all beside the point.

"Ayres, I want to borrow you. I mean, the Intelligence Department wants to borrow you from the air force—for an indefinite period, perhaps."

Dusty glanced impulsively at General Bradley. The air force chief nodded his head, but otherwise made no move. Nor did he say anything. When Dusty turned to Agent 10, his friend's face was a perfect blank. Suddenly Dusty chuckled.

"That's perfectly okay with me, sir," he said to General Horner. "But frankly, Lieutenant Horner and I have worked so often together that I've practically considered myself some sort of a stepchild of the Intelligence department."

"And valuable has been the service you have rendered the department," said the other seriously. "But this case is a little different. You will be entirely on your own. You can expect no help from us in case you get into trouble—such as being captured. Nor will you be able to admit your identity with the department to any of your friends.

"I can only explain it by saying, that it's a lone-wolf type of work. You will have less freedom and double the amount of responsibility. Once you leave on—on a mission—your chances of getting back will depend entirely upon you.

"In other words in the past you have helped us in a voluntary sort of way. Now you would be directly associated with us—our information would be your information, and your information would be ours."

Dusty grinned, half shrugged.

"It still doesn't strike me as being particularly different from what its been for months," he said. "But if it is—its perfectly okay with me."

General Horner didn't shoot out his hand, grab Dusty's and wring it warmly, meanwhile babbling words of gratitude and praise. As a matter of fact, he did nothing except nod. Then he pulled open a drawer of the desk and took out a small pellet of some kind of imitation wood.

It was no bigger than a medium-sized pea. Holding it between his thumb and forefinger he pressed it, half twisting at the same time. When he parted his fingers the two halves of the pellet rolled down into the palm of his hand.

One of the halves he dropped into a small box in the drawer.

The other he handed to Dusty, pointed his finger as the pilot scrutinized it intently.

"If I ever receive that from anyone but you, Ayres," he said in a steady voice, "I'll know that I can abandon all hope of ever seeing you alive again. You remember once finding a green bead in the shoe of one of our dead agents? Well, we have changed our system—we use those, now, instead of the bead.

"If you are captured, and are to be searched, swallow that half even if you do nothing else. It will dissolve in your stomach, and your captors will never know of your connection with the department."

Dusty stared at the half pellet. It was rounded, of course, on one side. The other side, the flat side, contained two tiny hairline grooves. He looked at General Horner, asked the question that instantly popped into his mind.

"Supposing this does get back to you, sir? How will you know it's mine?"

"Because it will fit exactly the half I am going to place in my secret files," was the prompt answer. "But God willing, I hope that you yourself will give it back to me—that I will receive it in no other way."

The seriousness of the others was not shared by Dusty. Somehow it all struck him as a new sort of game. A game played with death, to be sure. But hell! He'd been playing overtime periods with the Grim Reaper for months! Hooking up direct with the Intelligence department didn't change the rules much as far as he could see.

"Do I get a number, sir?" he asked before he realized how foolish the question sounded.

"Lieutenant Horner will acquaint you with all that sort of thing," replied the general. "He has arranged all that."

DUSTY'S EYES narrowed. So Jack Horner had known some of the answers all the time. He turned and gave his friend a wait-until-I-get-you-after-school look. The Intelligence ace simply shrugged, and said nothing. Dusty turned back to the senior officer as a new thought struck him.

"Naturally, I'm honored, sir," he hesitated. "But—well, I wonder if I'm qualified for the job? I can speak some of their lingo but I'm far from what you'd call proficient. There's lots of other tricks I guess I should know, too."

"Quite true," came the instant comment. "Intelligence work is a life occupation. None of us, I guess, becomes really and truly expert before we die—or get killed. But the circumstances alter your case considerably. Ayres—I'm going to give you the chance to volunteer for the most desperate and perilous undertaking ever attempted in this war. It is not an order, nor a request—simply an offer I'm putting up to you."

The general stopped either for emphasis, or to clear his throat. Dusty sensed the immediate arrival of the big moment of this strange meeting, and leaned forward, eyes riveted upon his senior officer.

"Yes sir? And it's—"

A wave of his hand completed the question. General Horner cleared his throat for the second time.

"It's an offer to help in the capture of Fire-Eyes!" he shot out bluntly.

Dusty blinked, swallowed a couple of times.

"Capture Fire-Eyes?" he began.

"Yes, capture him, kidnap him!" the other cut in. "And get him down here as our prisoner, alive."

Dusty whistled softly.

"Wow!" he breathed. "That is an assignment, and how! But, why try to kidnap him? Why not drill him with some ar-

JACK HORNER
AGENT "10"

mor-piercing slugs—some that will go through those so-called bullet-proof clothes he wears?

"Wouldn't that gain the same end? Your idea is to bust up the morale of the rest of them, isn't it? With their leader gone, they'd go haywire and so forth."

"Not entirely," the senior officer corrected. "Killing him might help—but capturing him alive, getting him down here, would help us a thousand times more.

"For one thing, we might be able to probe the mystery that surrounds the man. You must remember, Ayres, no one—not even his own followers, know who he is or anything about him.

"Good God, man, think what it would mean to us to be able to draw aside the curtain on all that? Hell, it would do more to the rest of the Blacks than all the shot and shells in the world!"

There was a lot of truth in General Horner's words, Dusty realized at once. But he also realized that it was a darn sight easier to shoot a man than to try and bring him back as a live prisoner from some point a couple of thousand miles away. Still, a job to be done, was a job to be done—and that was that.

"I guess you're right, sir," he said.

"I know I'm right! Look at it this way, too, Ayres. We know that Fire-Eyes has returned to this side of the Atlantic to renew what he left off when winter set in. Of what we know of the man's methods, his next blow at us will be something entirely different. Perhaps we can thwart it, as we've thwarted other blows.

"Anyway, our principal object in this war is to end it satisfactorily for the American people. Therefore, if we can nip the plans of Fire-Eyes in the bud, by nabbing the man himself, we will have traveled one hell of a long ways toward ending the war as we want it to end."

"Right, again, sir," Dusty nodded patiently. "So what are your plans? What do you want me to do? Naturally, I'm volunteering my services."

General Horner glanced toward his son, then back to Dusty again.

"That," he said slowly, "I leave entirely to you and Lieutenant Horner. The entire resources of this department and every other department are at your disposal. The lieutenant, I believe, has some sort of a tentative plan worked out. I must tell you, Ayres, that the original idea must be credited to him."

Dusty turned slowly toward Agent 10, gave him a long searching look tinged just a bit by an exasperated glare.

"So!" he grunted. "So Little Boy Blue is as much in the dark as I am, huh? He thought it up, all by himself, and he's all in the dark? Nuts!"

Young Horner grimaced, gestured with both hands.

"Now keep your shirt on, kid!" he said, as though they were alone instead of in the same room with two of the highest-ranking officers in Uncle Sam's armed forces. "It wasn't my place to say anything, then. And besides, knowing how you can bombard a guy with the damnedest questions, why I—"

The inter-department call-set buzzed harshly. General Horner reached out, snapped on contact, and announced himself. Every one in the room heard the words that came out of the small oval amplifier.

"Special emergency report from the Atlanta, Georgia, area, sir! The Twenty-fifth air concentration depot was completely destroyed fifteen minutes ago. All communication with the depot has been cut off.

"Signal H.Q. is now trying to make contact. No details available as yet. We received but one signal saying that the depot had been destroyed. This is Jordon, sir. Have either you or General Bradley any immediate orders?"

Seconds of tense silence, during which every eye was fastened on the communications unit. Then a low curse rumbled off General Horner's lips.

"Damn his hide! We're too late! He's already started it, blast him!"

He suddenly leaned forward, and put his lips close to the speaker unit.

"Try every way possible to make contact, Jordon!" he roared. "Try all adjacent areas. Use the emergency code call. I'll be right up there!"

And with that, the Intelligence chief leaped from his chair and went bounding toward the door. General Bradley, Dusty and Agent 10 were right at his heels as he dived through it.

CHAPTER 3
MIDNIGHT VOLCANO

"YOU'VE GOT to get through, Jordon! Hell man, there must be somebody alive down there!"

As General Horner barked out the words he stamped up

and down the steel-and copper-lined room atop the war department building. Communication instruments of all description filled the walls and a goodly portion of the floor.

Major Jordon, chief H.Q. signal officer darted from one instrument to another, twisted dial knobs, spun rheostats, and clicked innumerable switches.

Clamped over his head was a set of earphones. Long wire leads dangled down from them, looped up to a contact plug he held in his hand. He jabbed the plug into a hundred different sockets, did something with the recording dials each time, then shook his head and tried another socket.

At the far end of the room, standing with Bradley and Jack Horner, Dusty followed every movement of the Signal officer with brooding, anxious eyes. On two other occasions he had witnessed war drama taking place in this very room. And now he was a spectator for the third time.

The thought irked him. He couldn't stomach standing by and watching things happen. He wanted to do something himself, take a part in the proceedings—any part, just so long as he could be doing something.

But there wasn't anything to do. Major Jordon was doing all there was to do—and getting nowhere in his frantic efforts to contact some station within reach of the Atlanta depot.

Dusty pictured the place in his mind. He'd flown over it, and landed there, often. It was one of the biggest, if not the biggest, air depots in the country. It had once been stated that the Atlanta depot could handle a total of five thousand planes, and their personnel, without even straining its facilities. Dusty believed it. He'd seen the place too often with his own eyes.

And now it was destroyed. A great war-equipment center in smoke and shattered ruins? It seemed incredible—impossible.

On sudden impulse, Dusty walked over to General Horner, placed a restraining hand on his arm.

"There's one way we can find out, sir," and, with a shrug toward Major Jordon, "the quickest way, too, I guess."

The Intelligence chief was obviously too wrapped up in his own thoughts to get all of what Dusty said. He glared at him from under shaggy brows.

"What, what?" he boomed. "What are you talking about?"

"I said, sir, there's a quicker way to find out what's happened down there."

"Yes? And what's that way?"

"I saw one of those new high speed transports at the field when I landed," Dusty said. "I can get you down there in an hour, maybe less."

General Horner started to speak, but the sudden ticking of the teletype machine cut him off short. Everyone leaped toward the instrument, stared at the words as they were printed on the moving ribbon of paper.

S.C. Area to H.Q.—Radio communication impossible.... Entire area south static-jammed. Cause of Atlanta disaster not known.... Air patrol unable to get within a mile of the area. Everything in flames.... Rumored report is that Atlanta was destroyed from the air but no enemy aircraft sighted within five hundred miles…. Relief parties now trying to get through to stricken area. Further information later, if possible….

The clicking machine became silent at the end of the message. General Horner bent over the ribbon, obviously reading the message again. Then he glanced up at Major Jordon, looked at the wall panel of radio dials behind him. The signal officer shook his head sadly.

"That tells the story, general," he said bluntly. "I can't get anything but a static-jam howl. We'll have to depend on what they shoot us over the teletype. At least, for awhile."

The Intelligence chief growled something under his breath, turned to Dusty.

"All right, Ayres, come along," he snapped, starting toward the door. "Perhaps your way is the best. I've got to find out what happened there, some way."

Though Horner had spoken only to Dusty, both General Bradley and Agent 10 fell into step with them and followed them out to the express elevators. About thirty seconds later they were all in a staff car and roaring across Washington toward the military field.

Dusty was behind the wheel, and he slammed the car along at a whirlwind pace that made any kind of conversation impossible. One reason was because he kept the siren button jabbed down—evening had settled over the capital, and the other was because the occupants of the car were too busy hanging on to take time out for talking.

EVENTUALLY, DUSTY skidded the car to a full stop

in front of the operations office on the field. A few words from General Bradley, and the C.O. of the field set things humming.

A gleaming low-wing, twin-engined transport was rolled out to the line and made ready for flight in almost nothing flat. As soon as the last member of the party had climbed into the cabin, Dusty released the wheel brakes, and taxied out onto the two-way runway.

Floodlights drove back the shadows of night, and ramming open both throttles he sent the craft thundering down the smooth strip of concrete and pulled it up gracefully into the air.

THE INSTANT he was clear, he cranked the landing wheels up into the wing, banked around and set a dead-on course for the Atlantic area. Then he turned to General Horner seated beside him.

"You think this changes our original plans, sir?"

The other blinked at him.

"Eh? I don't know what you're talking about, Ayres."

"I mean, nabbing Fire-Eyes," Dusty explained. "You said something about being too late."

The general appeared to think it over awhile. Leaning forward he gazed silently out at the evening shadowed sky.

"Perhaps we are, and perhaps we're not," he grunted eventually. "This Atlanta business may not be true. But if it is—it means that he has already started. Destroying the Atlanta depot would be a major victory in itself."

"Ayres!" came General Bradley's voice, from the rear. "See if you can contact anything on the plane's set. It's one of the newest-type—can tune on any waveband."

"An idea, sir," nodded Dusty.

Clipping the phones over his ears, he snapped on contact and picked up the transmitter tube.

GEN. HORNER

"Calling all stations southeastern section!" he barked. "Official check-back requested on situation at Atlanta depot. H.Q. officials request—"

"What's the matter, Ayres?" General Horner growled as Dusty stopped short.

The pilot didn't pay any attention to the question. The dial needle on the incoming signal recorder was swinging back and forth and the tiny red bulb directly above it was blinking rapidly.

It meant that some station was sending out signals on a different wave-band than the one the transport's set was tuned in on. What's more, the sending station, wherever it was, was sending on a U.S. navy reading.

Slapping off transmission, Dusty spun the dial knob to the corresponding reading. Instantly the cabin speaker unit rattled out the clipped, excited sounds of a human voice.

"… to all coastal units! Warning to all coastal units! Second Atlantic battle squadron reports enemy aircraft flying high at AT-26, due south…. Type not confirmed. Believed to be bombers…. Scout planes launched unable to make contact before enemy aircraft had disappeared….

Estimated course slightly northwest from AT-26, south! All coastal units are advised to take air and maintain constant patrols…. Report all findings to your local headquarters…. Official! Second A.B.S. signing off…."

The speaker unit went silent. Dusty studied the roller map, made a few lightning-like calculations in his head then turned to General Horner.

"If they hold that course," he said, "they should pass us a bit to the east."

"Enemy bombers?" echoed the senior officer with a half snort. "They won't be passing us at all. Won't be able to. Our coastal patrols will take care of them.

"Besides, those navy lads on the water are always thinking they're spotting enemy aircraft. So if you've got an idea of swinging out toward sea, forget it! Get this damn thing down to Atlanta as fast as you can!"

IT SO happened that Dusty didn't have any such idea. He had only been impressed by the course that the "sighted" enemy aircraft were stated to be flying. When he did a little more calculating he suddenly realized that his first answer had been wrong. The enemy planes were flying a course that would take them directly over the Nation's capital.

He started to speak of that to General Horner, but the red signal light's blinking stopped him. The instant he spun the dial to the correct reading another voice came from the cabin speaker unit.

"All aircraft attention! Emergency signals from coastal Unit Forty…. Three squadrons of enemy aircraft bombers sighted ninety miles southeast of Chesapeake Bay…. Heading for Washington, D.C. Units Forty, Twelve and Seventeen now climbing to engage them…. All available aircraft concentrate on Washington, D.C. area…."

"By God, the blasted nerve of them! They don't stand a hope in hell!"

The shouted words from General Bradley's throat partially drowned out the last of the emergency call from Unit Forty.

"The damn fools!" the air force chief continued. "We've got a thousand planes to send up after them. Here, Ayres, let me get at that radio. Change seats with me, Horner. I'll make sure that those devils don't get away with anything so absurd as that! Not by a damn sight."

The two generals changed seats. Bradley fumbled with the ear-phones Dusty passed to him, finally got them adjusted and reached out his hand toward the transmission volume dial knob.

His fingers never touched it, though. His hand suddenly shot up, pointed toward the night-shadowed sky to the right.

"Look, look!" he got out in a choking gasp. "My good God—what's that? What's that damn thing?"

He need not have said anything. Every eye in the cabin was already fixed hypnotically on the night heavens high up to the right. For up there was a sight that chilled their bones to the marrow and made their throats go dry.

An uneven circle of phosphorescent, yellowish-red was floating down toward the ground far below. Like a smoke ring being struck by the air currents in a room, the weird circle continually changed its shape.

Now it was a perfect circle, now an oval, and now almost cross-like in form. Nor did all parts of it hold the same level. Like a gigantic ring of sea hawser floating on a heavy swell, it continually dipped down first on one side and then on the next.

All the time, tiny showers of crimson flame, like spatterings of molten metal, dropped down from its fringe to fall a few thousand feet or so before fusing out entirely.

Lower and lower it came. Then it seemed to hold the same altitude, and crab eastward as though being driven forward by a westerly wind at that level. Dully, Dusty was conscious of the fact that he was veering the transport away from the weird phenomenon.

It is almost as though he expected the thing to suddenly slide across the couple of miles of air space in between and loop itself around the transport. He was dully conscious also that he was cursing softly to himself, that the other three were mumbling sound, too. But if it had meant the saving of his life, he could not have torn his gaze from the fantastic sight.

Suddenly, though, as the thing went slip-sliding, half floating down below their level, and the initial shock at seeing it had passed away, he let out a howl that even startled himself.

"My God, do you know what's below that? The Virginia ammo depot—the ammo depot at Roanoke! The thing's going to settle on it! It'll wipe the dump out!"

"And us along with it!" came the booming cry from General Horner. "Get us away from here, Ayres! For God's sake, get us away from here. There's enough stuff down there to—"

INSTINCTIVELY, DUSTY twisted around in the seat. General Horner's mouth was open. He was trying to get words off his tongue, but they would not come.

Half slumped against the rear cabin air vent, he was trying to raise one hand—as though to attract somebody's attention. Agent 10 leaped toward him, started to help him back into a seat. But suddenly, he too went semi-rigid. General Horner slid out of his grasp, crumpled down onto the floor. A second later, Agent 10 went sprawling down on top of him.

"God! Something has happened to them!"

Dusty heard General Bradley's cry from a long, long way off. A strange buzzing had started up in his ears. His head seemed almost to detach itself from his shoulders and float away on its own.

43

In the dim light cast by the instrument board cowl lamp, he could see things—the instruments, his hands and legs, yet it was as though he was looking at them from a distance; as though they had no connection at all with his present position.

The buzzing in his ears had changed to a whirring hum. He saw his clenched right fist strike General Bradley's arm. He saw the air force head stare at him as though from a deep fog. Then he heard his own voice.

"Some—kind of gas! Coming—through cabin air vents! That handle—there! Turn it—close the vents!"

General Bradley didn't move. Dusty saw the man's muscles twitch. His brain managed to register the fact that the air force chief was trying to move, but was being held helpless in some horrible, paralytic grip.

Then Dusty realized that he wasn't looking at the air force chief any more. His eyes were fastened on the air-vent shutter handle on the man's right.

"You've got to do it—you've got to turn the damn thing yourself! Do it—do it before it's too late!"

HIS OWN voice was echoing around inside his head. He was half out of the seat. One hand was grabbing hold of General Bradley for support, the other was reaching out slowly for the vent handle. Bradley's eyes were still half opened. They were looking at him, and they held that dumb, mute appeal that one sees in the eyes of a domestic animal asking for help from its master.

The handle was six inches from the tips of his clawing fingers. God, but his head felt light! It hadn't been resting on his shoul-

THE VENT HANDLE WAS SIX INCHES FROM THE TIPS OF HIS CLAWING FINGERS

ders for hours. He must get that handle and turn it—close the incoming air vent, then snap up the "blower" switch for sucking all engine fumes out of the cabin. Maybe—maybe that would help. But first the damn vent handle. Ah—he had hold of it now.

He only knew that his fingers were twisting the handle because he could see them twisting it. There was no sense of feeling at all in his body. His muscles moved, still moved, but he could not feel them move.

Then his fingers stopped twisting, fell away from the vent handle. And he knew that they had twisted the vent shutters closed. He fell sprawling across General Bradley, slid off onto the floor of the pilot's compartment.

Inch by inch he raised himself up on one knee. Everything had become enveloped in a swirling fog. He saw instruments, buttons, switches, swim past in front of his eyes. One of them was the blower switch button. Ah—God be praised—he had his fingers on it!

Now—up with it! Snap it up! There—the blower had started. It was sucking the fog away. He knew it! He was beginning to see things clearly—beginning to feel life coming back to his lead-heavy muscles. His fumbling hand found the oxygen tank valve release. Ah, that was better! Now to get back into the seat. The old crate had slipped into a dive. He must have kicked the stabilizer adjustment lever with his foot when he fell over General Bradley.

At that moment, though, sky and earth split asunder. A volcano of roaring thunder and flame engulfed the transport. A battering ram straight from the pit of hell itself, smote the underside of the fuselage.

The jarring impact hurled Dusty clear of the seat, into which he was crawling, and flung him like a rag doll up against the instrument board. And then his brain exploded in a fountain of shooting stars.

CHAPTER 4
EAGLE'S PLAN

"WHAT IN God's name was happening," Dusty kept asking himself. Why was he falling through space? How had it all started, and where was he going?

"Steady, kid, steady! Up she comes! Bring her up out of this spin!" Dusty found both of his hands gripping the control stick. He was easing it back slowly. A side glance at the throttles showed that both had been retarded. The big plane was arcing smoothly up to even keel.

He laughed shakily. He had no memory of getting back into the seat. Nor could he remember retarding the throttles and starting to ease the stick back. Yet he had; his sub-conscious flying sense had directed him to do all those things. He sucked in his breath deeply. It made him giddy at first, but his brain cleared immediately afterward, and new strength poured back into his body.

A groan at his side brought his head around. General Bradley was mumbling, eyes closed, and weakly pushing himself up on the seat. The air force chief's face was deathly white. Every drop of blood under the skin had faded away. His movements were those of a man making a last desperate effort to drag himself back from the abyss of unconsciousness. Dusty hesitated a split second, then shrugged.

"You'll never know," he grunted. "And I think it'll help!"

With that he reached over with his free hand and smacked the palm against his superior's right cheek. Instantly General Bradley let out a sharp cry, twisted the upper part of his body, as though throwing off some great burden, sat up straight and opened his eyes wide. He blinked a couple of times then made a choking, gasping sound.

"Good God—what happened—where are we?"

"We're safe, I guess," Dusty answered. "And I don't know just what happened."

Then as the senior officer seemed to wilt, slide back into another coma—

"Get in back, sir! Help them, if you can. Try and bring them to. Slapping their faces will help—starts the blood circulating. Hurry up, sir!"

It was probably the first order that General Bradley had taken from anyone in months. But, let it be said to his credit, he didn't resent it, didn't even give Dusty a tough look. He simply nodded, climbed out of the seat and bent over the two Intelligence officers still sprawled out limply on the floor.

What he did to them, Dusty didn't notice. His own brain was now functioning at top speed, and he was directing his attention down at the ground. What he saw set his heart to pounding madly against his ribs.

About ten miles to his left, and down on the ground, there was a swirling ocean of light. A swirling storm-tossed ocean of conglomerate light. There were yellows, and blues, vivid crimson, tinges of green and purple. They kept merging together to form different hues, and from out of their midst great columns of brown smoke pillared upward.

As he stared at it he saw rockets of flame streak heavenward, leaving behind long tails of flickering sparks. Some of them mushroomed out in waterfalls of fire high in the sky. Others changed into mighty lightning-like flashes that cut the darkness for miles around, and then winked out. And through it all came a vibrating rumble and roar of sound.

HELD BY its eerie, horrible fascination, Dusty stared down at the panorama of hell's fireworks. He knew what it was, but he did not know what had caused it, other than that some weird, nocturnal phenomenon had floated down to completely encircle the Roanoke ammo depot and touched it off. Millions of shells of all calibre, countless powder magazines, Tetalyne storehouses and small-arms ammunition beyond estimate—had all exploded in one gigantic sea of flame and sound.

In spite of himself, Dusty shivered. He knew that Roanoke was the munitions center for the entire South. From it even the armies of the North and Eastern areas drew much of their supplies. Since the very first day of its establishment the ten-mile area had been guarded day and night on the ground and in the air.

For an American plane even to fly over it without special permission, meant a barrage of high-angle anti-aircraft guns that the pilot would never forget—assuming that he lived through it.

To approach it on the ground was to approach death, unless you were expected. The triple cordon shot you first, and established your identity later. Of all the war nerve centers in the entire United States, Roanoke was the solitary one that had never seen enemy agents within its borders.

And now—now it was no more. When daylight came, there would be nothing but a gigantic smoking crater. Roanoke gone—wiped from the very face of the earth!

"God Almighty—look at that—look down there!"

Even as Dusty turned around in the seat, he knew that the hoarse cry had come from General Horner. He saw the three of them, Bradley, Horner and his son, faces pressed against the side cabin windows, staring down at the ocean of fire. The reflection of the crimson glow tinted their strained faces, made them appear as three ghosts from some fantastic world.

The chief of Intelligence choked out a curse, turned half glazed eyes to Dusty.

"What happened, Ayres?" he asked thickly. "Why aren't we all dead?"

Dusty shrugged.

"Luck, sir," he grunted, "just plain luck. The other answers I don't know. The thing must have thrown off some sort of gas, though. It was sucked in through the air vents, that's what got you. If the cabin had been sealed, you'd have been all right."

General Horner swiveled his eyes around and down to the ocean of flame again, shuddered visibly.

"And if we'd have been a bit closer—" he said in a hollow voice, and stopped.

"We weren't, though," replied Dusty with forced cheerfulness.

"Hold tight, sir," he added. "I'm going to let this thing out for Atlanta, now."

"No, never mind going to Atlanta, Ayres!" the other cut him off. "Get us back to Washington as fast as you can. I'm needed there now."

Dusty didn't bother questioning his senior officer's sudden change of mind. Giving the horrible sight on the ground a final glance, he swung the craft around toward the Washington military field and opened up both engines.

During the ride back no one spoke. In fact, not until Dusty was taxiing the ship up to the line was the silence broken. General Horner broke it. He spoke to General Bradley.

"I'm going straight to Staff H.Q., Bradley. Are you coming along? I think you'd better. God knows but what this night'll mean a complete reorganization of supply bases. Yes, you'd better come along with me. You know how damn hard they are to handle at times."

"I'll come along," nodded the air force chief as Dusty braked the plane to a full stop.

Both generals immediately climbed down out of the cabin and hurried over to an empty staff car. Dusty made as though to follow them, but Agent 10 grabbed his arm, held him back.

"The sacred rooms of general staff are not for us, Dusty," he said. "We'd only just cool our heels, anyway. Let's take a turn up and down the tarmac and have a smoke."

The casual tone didn't fool Dusty for a single second.

"Okay," he grunted, and climbed down. "You supply the smokes—I've run out."

Agent 10 supplied a pack, held the match for them both. Then hands jammed in his tunic pocket he started walking along the tarmac, puffing furiously. Suddenly he turned his eyes toward Dusty.

"Nobody thanked you, kid, so I will," he said. "Your lungs must be made of leather."

"Huh?"

"Skip it! Bradley didn't close the vents and start the blower. Nor did he keep the plane in the air. That much I can figure. But—"

The Intelligence man stopped walking, faced Dusty squarely. Deep lines of worry creased his face.

"Any ideas?"

"About that?" Dusty echoed. "No, I haven't a damn one. That is, except that a ring of some kind of fire floated down. It threw off a curtain of mild gas—and we were damn near caught in it."

"But how did the thing get in the air?" Agent 10 shot at him. "You know that entire area is patrolled night and day. They have detectors, too, that are synchronized with the air patrol engines. So even though the Blacks tried to slip over in American planes they'd be nailed."

"Yeah, I know," nodded Dusty. "I'm thinking, though, of that navy emergency call we tuned in on."

"You mean those bombers did it?"

"No, I don't mean that. But it gives me an idea. Let's go find out what happened."

"Go where?"

"To the communications office here at the field, of course!" Dusty flung back over his shoulder as he started down the tarmac. "It was reported that those ships were headed for Washington. Looks like they gave it up. I'd like to know why."

A minute or so later Dusty shouldered through the door into the communications office. The signal captain in charge recognized him and grinned.

"Howdy, Ayres! What can I do for you?"

"Maybe plenty, Walker," Dusty replied. "You know Lieutenant Horner, of course."

"Yeah, sure," replied the other, shaking Jack Horner's hand. Then to Dusty, "Well, and so what?"

"That navy emergency awhile ago," Dusty said. "What happened to the enemy bombers that were supposed to be headed this way?"

The signal captain chuckled.

"The same thing that happens to all dopes who think they can slide in on us," he said. "Our coastal units met them, gave them a belly-full of steel and sent them high-tailing back to their carriers—must have been carriers.

"They faded out to sea, without dropping a single egg. A funny thing, though, one of them was forced down—near Dover, so the report came in. And it didn't have a single egg aboard!

"Well, what's new with you? Sore because you couldn't get in on the scrap? But say—I remember now—didn't I pick up a call of yours to all southeastern stations? Just before the first emergency came through? I'll swear that it was your voice."

DUSTY NODDED absently, said nothing. The germ of an

idea was spinning around inside his head. Captain Walker said something he didn't hear. He turned to Agent 10.

"No eggs aboard the crate forced down," he grunted. "Can you make anything of that?"

The Intelligence man looked puzzled.

"Maybe dumped them, just in case," he murmured.

"No bombs were dropped," spoke up Captain Walker, glancing from one to the other. "There wasn't a single report of a bomb being dropped. As a matter of fact, only two of them got in over the shore."

"Then that makes my idea wrong," said Agent 10. "What do you make of it?"

He directed the question at Dusty. The Yank ace didn't appear to hear, and turned toward the signal officer.

"Get any report on the condition of the ship?" he asked. "Cracked her up I suppose, huh?"

"Why no. As a matter of fact its being flown over here. Should be here soon, now. But why are you interested? Want it as a souvenir?"

"Maybe," Dusty grinned. "Well, thanks, Walker. We've got to be skipping along now. See you in the cemetery, sometime."

"Not me, you won't. S'long!"

"If it's okay with you," grunted Agent 10 when they were outside again, "would you please tell me about those thoughts I can almost see whizzing around inside that dome of yours?"

"Whizzing, is right," Dusty grinned tightly. "And not getting very far. Well, we know one thing, at least. The Blacks pulled every available crate of ours out to sea."

"How come?"

"No eggs on the bombers!" Dusty gestured. "That was a fake raid. Hell, do you think that if they didn't want to be seen that they'd fly low enough for surface ships to spot them?"

"Well—er—I suppose not. But what was the big idea?"

"I don't know," Dusty replied, scowling down at the tarmac. "But it might be so that something else could get in close to Roanoke. Maybe I'm wrong, but I'm willing to lay you a bet that before Atlanta went up in smoke, all patrol ships near it got an emergency call like the one we heard."

"But the regular patrol over Roanoke! They—"

"I said, get in close to Roanoke, not right over it!" Dusty cut him off.

Agent 10 grimaced.

"All right, go on from there," he said.

"Well, Walker didn't seem very excited," Dusty said to him. "And I must confess that I still am!"

"Nuts! For God's sake cut the riddles! What the hell are you getting at, anyway?"

"Just this, little boy!" Dusty shot at him. "The signal officer at the Washington military field, where one of our most powerful stations is located, doesn't know that Roanoke has been destroyed, yet!"

"Good God, that's right!"

"Go to the head of the class. No, make a guess first—why hasn't he heard?"

"Why—why because—"

Agent 10 cut himself off short, undecided.

"Because no message has been able to get through, so far," Dusty finished for him. "Which means that the thing we saw floating down, not only destroys whatever it touches, but at the same time throws off an electrical disturbance that static jams entire areas."

"Meaning that what we saw at Roanoke is what must have happened at Atlanta?" questioned young Horner.

"A close guess," nodded Dusty. Then added suddenly, "Listen Jack, I've a hunch that both things were merely preparation for something bigger. If we can get Fire-Eyes, maybe we can still stop it. What was the plan you'd thought up?"

"A gamble," replied the Intelligence man, "but it's one we've got to take. Dusty, Fire-Eyes is going to Bermuda. Now don't interrupt. I know that the Islands have been all knocked to hell. But I also know that he's making that a jumping off place.

"When he is due there, I don't know. Within the next day or so, though. I'm pretty sure. However, I've arranged for us to be taken out by submarine. We'll be a couple of Black sailors.

"The sub will set us adrift close to Hamilton harbor. There's a strong inshore current there that will carry us in. We're from the Black sub, X Thirty-five. She was sunk two days ago, off the Carolinas. We're the only two that were saved, see?"

"Yeah," grunted Dusty dubiously. "And just how do we get back—and bring Fire-Eyes with us?"

"The same way we went out," said Agent 10. "The Yank sub is going to be off Hamilton point every day just before dawn. I'm taking an infra-red buglight along to signal her if we want her to come in close. Naturally, when we get Fire-Eyes we've got to lay low until we can contact our sub. Can do someway, I guess."

"You're sure he's stopping at Bermuda?" Dusty asked. "I don't see why the hell—"

BIFF BOLTON

"Neither do I. But I got it straight from one of the best men in the department. Say, what's the matter?"

Dusty had suddenly started to pound one fist against the open palm of the other hand.

"Hell!" he said, "we can do it easier than that. Didn't you hear what Walker said—the bomber forced down is being flown over here. That's our meat—and a damn sight quicker than by submarine.

"Who knows but what Fire-Eyes might want to talk with a pair of pilots forced down during a fake raid. And after all, it'll be something for us to get away in in case we want to. Sure, its perfect! And we've wasted enough time. Can you get a couple of uniforms and your makeup kit?"

"Yes, but listen, Dusty—"

"Forget it!" Dusty cut him off sharply. "Don't you see, we can't waste the time in case you are wrong? But with that bomber we can go places—and Bermuda isn't the only one. And—look, that must be it coming in now!"

CHAPTER 5
MURDER DROME

THE FIELD siren had started to wail out its eerie note, and floodlights were springing into life. Presently the siren died out, and as it was lost to the echo Dusty heard the faint throbbing rhythm of throttled airplane engines to the east.

He turned, peered up into the sky, and saw half a dozen Yank pursuit planes come sliding down, settle gently on the tarmac and taxi into the hangar line. He only gave them a passing glance, though. There was still one more plane left in the sky. He watched it glide earthward.

"You're right, Dusty! It's the bomber they got at Dover!"

Dusty nodded at Agent 10's excited comment, said nothing,

and kept his eyes fixed on the plane. It was of the convention-al twin-engined, single center-winged type, with the folding landing deck trap-hook for use on airplane carriers. Its pilot was now cranking down the wheels. A moment or two later, the big craft touched the runway, rolled forward a few yards, and then was nosed around in toward the line.

When it came to a full stop, the door opened, and out piled a couple of Yank soldiers, each with drawn automatics. They waved them toward the open door and two figures in the uniform of Invader air force pilots stepped gingerly down onto the ground.

Their wrists had been shackled, and with a soldier taking up a position on either side they were herded through the group that had collected on the tarmac, and along it toward the field commander's office.

Dusty automatically started to join the group that trailed along behind, but suddenly stopped and grunted with surprise. Two other pilots in the uniform of the U.S. air force climbed out of the plane. Dusty blinked hard, took another good look, and started running toward the captured Black plane. Jack Horner also let out an astonished yip and stuck right at his heels.

"Well, I'll be damned!" roared Dusty, as he skidded to a halt in front of the pair. "What in hell are you two doing here?"

Curly Brooks turned and winked at Biff Bolton, jerked a thumb toward Dusty.

"Do you know this guy, Biff?" he asked. "Damned if that ugly mug of his doesn't look familiar! And who is the military fashion-plate with him?"

Bolton screwed up the features of his moon face, thoughtfully scratched a fingertip along his lower jaw.

"Gosh, you got me, Curly," he rumbled. "But they're always switching mechanics around to different fields you know. Maybe we've seen 'em at—"

The big pilot leaped to one side just in time to avoid Dusty's foot arcing up toward the seat of his breeches.

"Hey, don't!" he yelled. "I went horseback riding this morning!"

"Come on!" shouted Dusty. "What's the big idea?"

"Don't you ever listen in on the radio?" Curly answered for them. "My friend, you are now looking at two saviors of your country. Two gallant eagles of Uncle Sam, who heard a call to arms. With our trusty air steeds under us, we thundered to the scene of conflict. And there, by dint of courage, grim determination, and flying skill you'll never be able to acquire—my valiant comrade and I convinced a couple of Black clucks that it would be one hell of a good idea for them to set their lousy crate down on the ground and call it a day!"

"And figuring that you might be here, and need taking home," added Biff Bolton, "we got permission to fly the crate over. And of course we brought those two yeggs along for your department to play with, Jack."

"You mean you were mixed up with those bombers that were reported to be headed this way?" Dusty frowned.

"Yeah, sure," Curly nodded. "Biff and I were joy-hopping around Atlantic City when we tuned in the call. So we slammed on down, just for the hell of it. Must admit, though, that we were only two of about nine hundred crates that showed up. But, we were lucky, though. Got the only bomber. The rest beat it, with some of our lads after them. This baby here didn't like the looks of our X-Diesels, I guess. He just quit, and we followed him down."

"You got the call too, huh, skipper?" asked Biff. "I didn't see your ship."

"Didn't have a chance to get over," Dusty replied evasively.

"Ah-h-h!" breathed Curly softly. Then, "Mama tell papa all about it, huh?"

"If you insist," said Dusty evenly. "Atlanta and Roanoke have been completely wiped out!"

Curly and Biff stiffened, and the kidding grins on their faces vanished immediately.

"What?" they roared in the same breath. "When? How?"

CONSCIOUS OF the look of annoyance that came into Jack Horner's eyes, Dusty told them of the flight of the transport plane. But that was all, much to young Horner's evident relief. It was Curly who broke the silence that followed Dusty's words.

"I was wondering," he grunted. "I couldn't figure why this baby, here, had no eggs aboard. And I didn't see any on the others either. But you haven't any idea what—what that thing could have been?"

Dusty shook his head.

"Not the faintest," he grunted. Then he added in a sharper tone, "Well, its been nice seeing you children again. Now get

HE HELD IT UP FOR THE OTHERS TO SEE.

back to your ships, and get along home before the major docks you a month's pay."

Neither of them moved. Curly fished for a cigarette.

"Coming along with us, kid?" he murmured casually to Dusty. Dusty shook his head.

"Can't! Jack and I have got—"

A pistol shot suddenly shattered the stillness of the night. Before it was lost to the echo, the piercing cry of a man in mortal pain rang out. The sound came from Dusty's right, over by the radio building, some hundred yards away.

In a flash he spun around, jerked his automatic free and started pounding over the ground, the three others right at his heels. When he was still fifty yards from the radio building, he saw the door slam open. Before he could even swing up his gun, a figure darted out and immediately lost itself in the surrounding darkness.

From out of that darkness a sentry bellowed, "Halt!" And his rifle spat flame and sound. A couple of other sentries roared out a challenge too, and followed it up by pulling triggers. As a matter of fact, in the space of split seconds the entire field was in an uproar.

Officers and men were dashing out of buildings and hangars. Someone was roaring for the floodlights to be turned on; someone else was bellowing for the sentries to form a cordon about the field.

Dusty, however, did not check his pace toward the radio building. When he reached it, he dived in through the door, skidded to a halt, and snapped his eyes about the room.

The first thing he saw was a bullet shattered transmitter unit on the far wall. Then he saw the feet and lower part of the legs of a man on the floor behind an overturned table. Darting around the table he bent over the limp figure of a Yank radio sergeant.

The non-com's right hand held a service automatic. The arm had been flung out so that the gun was resting on the floor. His eyes were closed, and his O.D. shirt just above the place where his heart would be was stained a dull crimson. As Dusty reached out a hand for the man's pulse, the non-com coughed raspingly and blood spattered off his lips.

"Lousy Black rat—use my set will you? I'll damn well—"

The voice trailed off to an unintelligible whisper. Dusty bent his head low.

"Who was it, sergeant!" he called out. "How do you know he was a Black? What happened?"

The radio non-com stared at him through glassy eyes, seemed to realize that he was a Yank.

"Gone for a bite," came the gasping words. "Found—the rat trying to contact Black station—on low wave-length. Shot—and busted transmitter. He—he slung knife—the dirty—"

THE EFFORT was too much. The man's words became a horrible gurgling sound in his throat. By that time, Curly, Jack Horner and Biff Bolton had joined Dusty. But all four of them were equally helpless to do anything for the radio man. He was beyond all possible help. A final sigh slid off his lips and he died.

For a moment or two Dusty continued to stare at him. Then

on impulse he reached down and pulled a small bone-handled trench knife from under the dead man. The blade was covered with fresh blood. He held it up for the others to see, then let it drop to the floor again.

"Good God!" young Horner choked, "what do you suppose?"

"Plenty!" Dusty snapped getting to his feet. "Curly! Biff! Tear out and help them catch the bum who did this. Hurry up—get going! Jack—you stick here a second!"

Curly and Biff hesitated a moment, then ducked outside. Young Horner immediately turned to Dusty, but the Yank ace silenced him with a gesture.

"Now I'm getting ideas!" he said in a low, hurried voice. "And it's that that bomber is important. The Blacks didn't plan on it being captured. The rat who killed this poor devil tried to tell someone about the bomber—that its crew had been captured. Anyway, you and I are leaving in it at once.

"That bomber is our homing pigeon. I'm sure of it. It's going to take us right to the center of this mess. I'm going to do a little signaling with it on my own. Tell you about it later. Listen, those two pilots that were captured. They took 'em to the guard house. Go over and get their uniforms and your make-up kit. And meet me in the bomber on the far side of the field in ten minutes. Can do?"

"Yes, sure!"

Dusty started pushing him toward the door.

"Tell you about it later, Jack!" he snapped. "I'm betting everything I ever had that I'm right. Now, get going!" Young Horner hesitated, took a last look at the dead radio sergeant, then went bounding out the door. When Dusty left a couple of moments later, there was a steely glint in his eye. A crowd had collected in front of the open door, and several questions were hurled at him. To them all he shrugged.

"I don't know a thing!" he snapped. "You, corporal, stand guard. Someone go get the field C.O. You two, there, come give me a lift with the bomber. I'm going to fly it to Dayton for examination!"

He said the last in a loud voice, and let his eyes slide over the group. Was one of them the rat who killed the radio sergeant? It stood to reason that the man was garbed in a Yank uniform. There was no answer to the question, and with two mechanics at his heels, he ran over to the bomber, climbed into the pilot's compartment and started the twin engines. As they roared into life he thought that he heard a few more rifle shots. He wasn't sure, and didn't stop to investigate. Giving the mechanics the nod to stand clear, he slowly taxied over to the far side of the field.

It seemed that he had no sooner reached the other side, swung around into the wind, than a figure ran out of the darkness, jerked open the cabin door, and climbed inside.

"Fast work, Jack!" Dusty started, then stopped short.

The grinning figure, black pilot uniforms slung over his arm, who slid into the seat beside him, was Curly Brooks!

"You! What the hell?"

"Yeah!" Brooks came back sharply. "Get the hell off! I'll tell you about it."

"Listen, Curly, no—"

"Off, Dusty, for God's sake!" the other rapped at him. "Jack has been wounded—not seriously. But he can't join you! Now get this damn thing into the air!"

CHAPTER 6
ONE DOWN, TWO TO GO

DUSTY HESITATED for a fraction of a second, then rammed home both throttles and sent the Black bomber roaring across the field. Once he got it clear and headed up into the night sky, he snapped on the instrument cowl lamp and turned to Curly.

"Let's have it, quick!" he snapped. "What happened?"

"Knew there was something up," began Curly, speaking rapidly. "So I hung near the radio hut, joined Jack when he came out. He wouldn't say a thing. But I went into the guard room with him. The general was there, working on those two Blacks. Listen Dusty, they came through. One of them 'fessed up that Fire-Eyes left this afternoon by submarine for Bermuda. He's due there at dawn."

"What?"

"Right! Due there at dawn. I heard that much. Then Jack collected their uniforms and started out. It happened then—a dumb guard opened fire before either of us could stop him. The damn fool winged Jack in the shoulder. Jack told me he was to meet you. So I took the uniforms and came on—his kit, too. He said to be sure to tell you about Bermuda. We head there, now, eh?"

"Maybe," grunted Dusty, frowning. "But I'm going alone. Listen, Curly, don't ask questions—but you can't come. Dammit, you don't know the language."

"Nuts, I don't! After listening to you recite your lessons out loud for the last three weeks, I could tackle Chinese in nothing flat. I learned enough to get me by in a pinch. Whatever your plan is, you can do most of the talking. I'll just act like a dumb guy—make believe I'm Dusty Ayres."

As Curly talked he was busily peeling off his uniform and climbing into one of those he brought along. That done, he went to work on his face with Jack Horner's make-up kit. Dusty said nothing, but his brain was clicking over at lightning-like speed.

He was both glad and angry that Curly was along. Brooks was the best man in the world to have along when it came to trouble. Yet, this was a job where a second man might prove a hindrance rather than a help. Before leaving the radio building, he had noted the wave-length reading on the outgoing message recorder. Once he got altitude he was going to contact that wave-length himself. The station direction-finder dial, when he received a check-back would tell him plenty—he hoped.

"Here, I'll take over while you change."

Curly's voice cut in on Dusty's thoughts. Reluctantly he turned over control of the plane, and started changing his own uniform for the one Curly had brought along for him.

"Is it Bermuda?" Brooks asked. "And what do we do?"

"Yeah, it is," Dusty grunted. "But first I'm going to play with this radio a bit. I'll take over, now. You dump our stuff out the window, when I bank. Don't want them to catch in the tail section."

Curly had dumped the Yank uniforms, and Dusty was reaching for the radio set, when it happened.

"Fly straight north! Don't move—either of you!"

Dusty froze, held his breath. It didn't, however, require the psychic powers of a fortune teller to figure out the situation. The owner of the gun suddenly jabbed against the back of his neck was the murderer of the radio sergeant.

Failing in his plan to contact someone, the man had done what any other quick-thinking spy would have done—hidden himself where the searching party would least expect to find him.

For a split second the pressure of the gun on Dusty's neck was released. He heard Curly sigh, and out of the corner of his eye saw his pal slump over limp against the side of the cabin.

"Damn you—"

"Steady! Fly north, I say!"

Raging inwardly, but quite conscious of the gun back in his neck again, Dusty altered the course of the bomber from due east to north.

A grating chuckle greeted his movements.

"This is one time you cannot talk yourself out of it, my friend! I am not so stupid as the others!"

Dusty shrugged but made no effort to open up the throttles.

"Talk myself out of it?" he snorted. "Hell, think I'm a dummy—that gun of yours in my neck? But you didn't get word through to your boy friends after all, eh? Too bad that radio sergeant wasn't a better shot."

The pressure of the gun against Dusty's neck wasn't relaxed a single bit.

"The throttles, my friend," said the figure in back. "I'm in a hurry. Open them up to full power."

DUSTY'S HEART sank. With a sigh he reached out his free hand toward the throttles, shoved them forward. But as he brought his hand back he allowed it to hit against the cabin light switch. Instantly the cabin was flooded with light. The man in back of him cursed harshly, jabbed the gun forward so savagely that Dusty had to grit his teeth hard to check the groan of pain coming up to his lips. "Turn off that light," came the hissing words, "or you will die!"

"Okay, sorry," Dusty grunted, his heart pounding wildly. "My mistake."

"Another mistake will be your last."

Dusty leaned forward, flicked off the light switch, but a tiny grin tugged at the corners of his mouth. In the few seconds allowed he had obtained a good look in the rear view mirror fitted to the top of the instrument board. In that mirror he had seen the reflection of the steel-eyed figure in the uniform of a U.S. air force mechanic, standing behind him.

More important that that, though, he had noticed that the man wore no parachute pack, nor were there any parachute packs on the rack farther back in the cabin. In other words, the only parachute aboard the plane was the vest pack clamped to the back of the seat in which Dusty sat.

"TURN OFF THAT LIGHT OR YOU DIE!"

With the knowledge of that, hope sprang up anew in Dusty's breast. The Black agent had not pulled the trigger of his gun because he was not a pilot, and there was no way of safely leaving the plane. To get the vest pack, against which Dusty leaned, would necessitate Dusty's taking his hands from the controls and getting out of the seat. It was kismet for fair.

For a couple of minutes neither man spoke. Holding himself rigid, Dusty weighed his chances of risking a bullet in the back of the neck. There was the ever present possibility that the Black might go haywire and let him have it anyway. If he could only figure on some way to get that gun away from his neck—get it away for just a couple of split seconds.

The voice behind him broke into his spinning train of thought.

"Don't move my friend! I am going to use the radio!"

A hand reached around in front of Dusty, snapped on radio contact, and spun the wave-length dial. The dial needle moved down a reading well below the general transmitting wave-length. In fact, way down to the reading Dusty had noted in the Washington field radio building. Then the Black reached over and picked up the transmitter tube and the head phones. Swiftly and silently Dusty tensed his whole body. He didn't know whom the Black was planning to contact. But he could make a wild guess. Maybe he was wrong—but he couldn't risk it.

"You poor boob!" he snapped. "Think you can send on such low transmitting volume?"

There was a grunt behind him. Again the hand reached around in front of him, and toward the radio panel. Without seeming to move, Dusty hunched his shoulder against the upper part of the Black's arm. The man stretched his arm a bit more and for a fleeting instant the pressure of the gun muzzle against Dusty's neck was relaxed.

In that infinitesimal period of time, Dusty whirled into action. With every ounce of his strength he slammed down on the left rudder pedal, belted the stick over, and ducked his head forward. The plane lurched to the left, and the Black, whose weight was on his right foot, was flung off balance to the right.

He roared out a curse in his native tongue, tried to swing his left hand holding the gun down toward Dusty, But his lurch to the right had pulled the gun too far back. And when it spat flame and sound, the hunk of steel from its muzzle chewed into the left side of the cabin.

He didn't have time to jerk the trigger twice. One hundred and eight-five pounds of American wildcat was upon him. The instant Dusty slammed the plane into its split-arc turn to the left, and ducked forward, he pivoted about and hurled himself out of the pilot's seat.

While still practically in mid-air, he got a flash glance of the Black toppling over backward, and of the flame-spitting gun clenched in his left hand. Then Dusty dropped down. One hand caught the Black by the throat. The other clamped down on the gun hand wrist. And Dusty's knee plowed down on the Black's stomach.

Air whistled hoarsely from the agent's twisted lips. The skin of his face went purple. His veins stood out taut, and his steely eyes bulged from their sockets and became glassy.

Twisting sharply over on his side Dusty crashed down with

his right foot a split second after he let go of the man's gun wrist. Wrist bones crunched under his heel and the gun dropped out of limp fingers. Pivoting back, Dusty swung his clenched free fist and clouted the Black on the left temple.

The Black gave up the ghost then. His eyelids fluttered closed. His tongue sagged out one corner of his mouth and his whole body went limp as a sack of rain-soaked grain.

Heaving himself up, Dusty grabbed the gun on the cabin floor, and dropped back into the pilot's seat. It took him a second or two to pull the plane back on even keel, swing it around and head it due south. Then he swung on robot control.

"Now, sweetheart," he breathed heavily, "it's papa's time to draw cards!"

Getting out of the seat, he bent over and jerked the Black up onto his feet. Holding him pressed against the wall with one hand, so that his drooping head was propped up, he began systematically to smack first one cheek and then the other with the flat of his hand. The Black's face was dripping blood before he finally opened his eyes.

Dusty stopped smacking him, waited for the man's brain to clear. Presently the glazed look in the man's eyes faded out to be replaced by a glare of berserk hatred. He ran his tongue over his bleeding lips, tried to shift his weight on his feet. But Dusty held him fast.

"Who talked who out of it that time, eh?" he clipped at the man. "Looks to me like you're the sucker."

THE BLACK mumbled something hoarsely, but it was too jumbled up for Dusty to understand any of it. With a sudden movement he released his hold on the Black, stepped back. The agent wasn't prepared, and he sat down as though he'd been smacked across the back of the knees.

A gurgling roar spilled off his lips, and he started to get up. But that's all he did—just started. Dusty's hand, holding the gun, snaked out and slashed down. Blood spurted from the man's ear to the point of his jaw, and he let out a scream of pain.

"That's better!" Dusty grinned, as the other remained seated on the floor. "I don't like to talk to people when they're standing up."

Cobra eyes glittered into his.

"Shoot me—I will tell you nothing! Nothing at all."

The words were little more than a continued hiss of sound. Dusty shrugged, fingered the gun he held in his hand.

"Not even a teeny-weeny little bit?" he echoed.

The Black spattered blood, as he shook his head savagely.

"Kill me—but I will not say anything!"

Dusty's lips were frozen in a half grin, but his eyes were stone cold, emotionless.

"Dead rats don't talk," he said in an even deadly voice. "I'd be a sucker to kill you. I'm just going to ask you to change your mind. But just keep your shirt on. I want my pal to listen in on this."

Swinging on robot control, Dusty kept the Black covered, reached over and slapped Curly's face. Brooks groaned weakly and raised a protesting hand. Then his eyes opened and he stared dully about. He didn't get it at all, at first.

"What the hell?" he mumbled.

Then he saw the Black and his right fist cocked back.

"Hold it, Curly!" Dusty stopped him. "The company wants to talk. You okay, now?"

"Yeah, guess so. How'd you do it?"

Dusty grinned, turned toward the Black. His gun hand shot out. The man saw it coming and tried to duck. He was about five and a half years too late. The down-slashing gun muzzle opened his left cheek some more, and his scream of pain made Dusty's ear-drums ring.

"Don't—don't!"

"That's up to you, sweetheart," Dusty said to him in a soft, yet deadly voice. "Now, the first question—who were you trying to contact at the Washington field, huh? Speak up—we haven't got all night!"

The Black sunk his teeth deep into his lower lip, and said nothing. Dusty leaned forward.

"Shall I tell you?" he barked. "It was Fire-Eyes, wasn't it? Fire-Eyes on his way to Bermuda, eh? Now, tell us why he's going there? No, first tell us about what happened at Atlanta and Roanoke? What was it?"

The man shook his head vigorously, spattered blood from his slit cheeks.

"I don't know!" he moaned. "I don't know!"

Dusty shot a glance at Curly, read the mutual thought in his pal's eyes. The Black was undoubtedly telling the truth—he didn't know.

"Where is the attack to be made?" he suddenly shot at the man.

"I—tell you—nothing!"

Dusty raised the gun again, then as a new thought suddenly hit him with dynamite force he unconsciously lowered the gun, half turned toward the radio.

"Dusty—look out!" Curly's cry jerked Dusty around. He didn't have time to do anything but pull the trigger. The Black, cornered like a rat, was making a last desperate attack. And it was his last attack, too.

The bullet smashed squarely between his eyes, and he was stone dead even as he fell on top of Dusty. With a heave, the Yank shoved him off, and let him drop flat on the floor.

"Too bad," he grunted, "but it checks with my idea."

"What idea?" asked Curly. "I didn't think he said much."

"Didn't," Dusty replied. "It's what he did—I'm just getting stupid."

"Say, what the—"

"Pipe down, and look at the radio, Curly," Dusty interrupted. "See, it's not on a ground station wave-length, nor a navy one either."

"By God, no!" Brooks gasped. "He was trying to contact some plane in the air!"

"Right!" Dusty nodded. "That bum was going to send some message through to a plane. I'm wondering, Curly—I'm wondering if Fire-Eyes is on his way to Bermuda by submarine. Anyway, we're going to start finding out things right now!"

Slipping on the ear-phones, he reached out his other hand to twist on full transmission volume.

"Here's where you test your knowledge of the lingo, kid!" he breathed softly. "Better make it good!"

A moment or two to suck in his breath and steady himself. Then he put his lips to the transmitter tube.

"Are my signals clear?" he asked in the harsh grating jargon of the Black Invaders.

Seconds of tingling silence ticked past. Every nerve and muscle in his body quivered with excitement. His hand holding the transmitter tube shook so violently that he had to jam it against his lips. Suddenly, there was a buzzing sound in the ear-phones. Then a voice answered in the same tongue.

"Signals clear! Make report in code, quickly!"

HAD THE wings dropped off the plane at that moment, Dusty would have not been any more surprised. Wide-eyed he stared at the radio panel, oblivious to Curly's questioning gaze. His heart looped over inside his chest. And his surging blood roared in his ears. Even though the words had come to him in the native tongue of the Black Invaders, he recognized the voice instantly.

It had been the voice of Zytoff, the Black ace of aces, and his greatest enemy.

"Your report in code! Quickly, fool!"

The sound of Zytoff speaking again jerked Dusty out of his whirling trance. He gulped, snapped his eyes toward the station direction finder. And it was then that he received the second jolt in as many minutes. Zytoff was not more than four hundred miles from his present position. As a matter of fact the Black's position was half way between the Delaware coast and Bermuda.

And unless the station direction-finder was going haywire, he was flying a course straight for Bermuda!

"Your report!" the ear-phones crackled.

Impulsively Dusty jerked the transmitter tube back to his lips.

"Impossible at present," he said. "Enemy has discovered key symbol. But they suspect nothing of plans. Call you back soon. Signing off!"

"Wait!" barked the ear-phones. "Maintain your contact! What is your code number?"

Dusty thought quickly, remembered that Jack Horner had once told him that Black agents were listed by a number preceded by the letter B.

"B Three-sixteen!" he snapped. "Enemy planes approaching. Signing off!"

As he spoke he tuned down transmission volume to give Zytoff the impression of set failure. Then he snapped off contact altogether, and turned to Curly.

"That dead Black there was important!" he shouted. "The Blacks are waiting for something—something that bird planned to tell them. Listen, Curly, it's perfect—Zytoff is Fire-Eyes' right hand man. We'll hook onto him.

"Wherever the attack is, it's a cinch Zytoff will be there. And Fire-Eyes will be with him. I knew damn well this crate would take me to the center of things. Listen, we're over water—dump that dead Black! We don't want him around in case we have to land."

"But I still don't get it!" Curly exclaimed as he got up from his seat. "I heard him ask you for the report, but—"

"Exactly the idea!" Dusty cut him off. "He wants a report about something I don't know. But get this—and I've figured it so right from the start—Zytoff was behind what happened at Atlanta and Roanoke. So we tag him and he'll lead us right to the front stoop of Fire-Eyes, whether it's Bermuda or Reno. Get going with that Black."

Leaning forward, Dusty snapped on radio contact and twisted on full transmission volume. The wave-length reading he didn't touch, for it was still the same.

"B Three-Sixteen checking back!" he called in the Black Invader tongue. "Contact for special report!"

Ripples of tense excitement chasing up and down his spine, he waited for the reply, eyes glued to the station direction finder. A moment and the ear-phones crackled so loud that they both heard it.

"No report, now! Proceed at once for enemy naval engagement at AT-Twenty-two!"

The voice clicked off into silence. Brows furrowed in a puzzled frown, Dusty continued to stare at the station direction finder dial. According to the dial, Zytoff had changed his course. In fact he had done a right about face and was flying back toward the American coast. As a matter of fact he was within shooting distance of the Delaware shore. And then Dusty let out a bellow of surprise.

"Hell yes! The naval arsenals south of Wilmington!"

He shouted the words at the top of his voice, and kicked the ship around in a groaning left bank. Curly reached over and grabbed his arm.

"What the hell!" he asked. "What are you changing our course for?"

"I got it now!" yelled Dusty, as though he were talking to himself. "Sure! It's Wilmington next!"

"But why? What about the naval engagement at AT-Twenty-two?"

"Don't you savvy it?" Dusty barked back. "AT-Twenty-two is about four hundred miles off the New Jersey coast! A naval scrap there would pull all available ships away from the seaboard bases and leave Wilmington wide open. Hell, Curly, figure it out—Atlanta, Roanoke, and now Wilmington!"

"By, God, yes!" Brooks cut in. "Our three most important bases along the east coast!"

"Right! And—"

The red signal light on the radio panel blinked rapidly. As Dusty shot out his free hand, he noted that some station was sending out signals over the U.S. navy S.O.S. wave-length. A couple of seconds later, when he'd spun the dial knob, the broadcaster's voice barked in the earphones.

"Third and Fourth Atlantic squadrons! Attention Third and Fourth Atlantic squadrons…. Strong enemy naval force reported north of AT-Twenty-two Area…. Proceeding southwest in battle formation…. Proceed and make contact at once. All naval and coastal air units within range are hereby ordered to support this maneuver."

The words smacked against Dusty's ear-drums, whirled

around inside his head. He hesitated for the fraction of a second, then snapped on full transmission volume and grabbed up the transmitting tube.

"Air units, Delaware area, attention!" he roared into it. "Believe enemy plans to attack Wilmington naval base. Advise constant patrol over entire area!"

"You poor boob!" Curly shouted as Dusty signed off. "Don't you suppose that he'll listen in on that?"

"I hope to God, he will!" Dusty cracked back. "It may make him change his mind. May make him realize that we're onto his little trick. Hang on—with luck we should meet him about half way between the Delaware coast and AT-Twenty-two!"

CHAPTER 7
ATLANTIC TORNADO

B OTH PROPS spinning over at maximum revs, Dusty held the plane on a crow's course for a point far out over the Atlantic. To the east, dawn was etching a thin line of light along the horizon.

For an hour neither Dusty or Curly spoke a word. There was nothing for them to say. What they expected to meet, neither of them had the faintest idea. Perhaps full dawn would see the greatest naval battle in history. Or perhaps it would see hundreds of Yank and Black Invader planes fighting for supremacy of the air above the east coast of the nation.

Of one thing, though, they were positive. The enemy was preparing to strike its master blow. Maybe by air, maybe by water—and maybe by both. With Atlanta and Roanoke destroyed, the American military resources were badly crippled. If Wilmington were destroyed too—

Dusty refused to think of the answer. Hunching forward over the stick he kept switching his gaze from the radio panel to the shadowy skies ahead. Not once, however, did the red light on the panel blink. Realization of that added to his worries.

By all rights, a hundred-and-one navy messages should be streaking through the ether. The Third and Fourth Atlantic squadrons should be communicating their progress back to navy H.Q. That, of course, would be done by code. But, the signals would register on the radio nevertheless.

Impulsively, Dusty reached out and twisted the dial knob so that the needle touched every available wave-length reading. Yet, not once did the red light flash its signal.

"The set's gone on the blink," he grunted to himself. "Or else they—"

It was then that he heard it. A faint high-keyed hum in the phones. His heart stood still, as he swung around toward Curly.

"No wonder!" he shouted aloud, unhooking one of the phones and pressing it against Curly's ear. "Everything's been static-jammed!"

Curly nodded dully.

"That makes it just as tough for them!" he replied. "They can't get anything through, either."

"Maybe they don't have to!" Dusty snapped.

"Good God—look there!"

Curly's sharp cry was but an echo in Dusty's ears. Far ahead the dawn sky had suddenly been transformed into a gigantic whirlpool of yellowish-red flame. Rather, it was not one whirlpool, but a dozen or more of them. A dozen or more circles of fire cutting down toward the rolling waters of the Atlantic.

In a flash, dark skies flared up into the brilliance of high noon. Like a curtain being drawn aside from the window of a lighted room, the entire eastern heavens shimmered in dazzling light.

For a second or two it all blinded Dusty. Then, as the retina of his eyes became adjusted to the sparkling glare, he saw a unit of U.S. carrier planes become engulfed in swirling hell. Like flies caught in the heat of a blast furnace, the American naval planes seemed to shrivel up and go plunging down, leaving behind long trails of oily black smoke. Some of them were completely encircled by the flaming whirlpools, and like tinfoil they virtually melted away into nothing.

Unable to speak, or even make a sound, Dusty unconsciously glanced downward. Far below, the water was dotted with Yank ships of all types. Black smoke poured from every funnel, and Dusty could almost see the foamy waters churned up by spinning propellers. And at that moment a whirlpool of hell slithered down from above, and completely ringed four armored cruisers.

Instantly great clouds of sooty steam belched skyward to completely hide the cruisers from view. And as though hell itself were exploding by sections, great fountains of livid flame spouted up through the blanket of billowing steam.

A moment later, another whirlpool swept down to ring six

sleek torpedo destroyers. Like the armored cruisers they became lost in flame and sooty steam. Another whirlpool came down, and another, and another, until it looked as though the entire Atlantic was one limitless expanse of raging flame.

From a thousand miles away, Dusty faintly heard his own voice. Then he became conscious of the fact that Curly was pounding him with one hand, and pointing off up to the right with the other. Then Brooks' words broke through his own shouted curses.

"Up there—there's a ship up there! See it? See it? Not a Yank ship either!"

Dusty twisted around in the seat, put up one hand to block the glare as much as he could, and strained his eyes in the direction Curly pointed. About five thousand feet above his own altitude, and perhaps five miles farther out to sea, a lone plane was drifting about in a series of lazy circles.

The distance was too great to see details clearly but Dusty was able to note the biplane wings with back-to-back engines set between the wings, halfway out from either side of the fuselage.

On top of the fuselage, at a point where the top wings joined it, there was what looked to be some sort of a turret arrangement. He wasn't sure, but he thought that the muzzle of a high-calibre gun projected out from the turret.

Before he had time to get a good look, another diving whirlpool of flame appeared in the air about half a mile directly in front of him. Its brilliance instantly blotted out the strange craft overhead.

With a wild cry he slammed down on right rudder with every ounce of his strength. And at the same time he shoved the stick over. The bomber virtually groaned aloud in protest against the violent maneuver. But it was no time to think about being gentle with the plane. Like a nail being drawn toward a powerful magnet, the floating ring of fire was sweeping down toward them.

"We'll never make it—it's going to get us!"

Dusty made no attempt to reply to Curly's shout of alarm. The interior of the cabin had suddenly become as the interior of a blast furnace. Sweat oozed out on Dusty's forehead, trickled down into his eyes.

Through half-glazed eyes he stared at the sealing lugs of the cabin, noted dully that they were twisted in place. Instinctively though, he held his breath. Memory of Roanoke caused him to do that.

Engines roaring out their song of over-revved power, the bomber went hurtling downward. Each split second was a lifetime in hell to Dusty. No matter how fast the bomber tore down, the whirling ring of yellowish red fire appeared to go faster. It grew bigger and bigger, its edges widening out across the sky.

"Hang on tight!" Dusty gasped. "Our only hope is to zoom up past—before it gets over us!"

EVEN AS he got out the words he pulled the stick back, straightened the rudder. With an ungodly wail that must have been heard way into shore, the nose of the bomber arced up toward the heavens.

...THE BOMBER SKIDDED OUTWARD AND UPWARD IN A VERTICAL POSITION

A split second later Dusty shoved down on the right rudder pedal, pushed the stick over. Like some giant bird caught in a terrific side wind, the bomber skidded outward and upward in a vertical position.

To the left a whirlpool of fire was sweeping toward him. Unable to do any thing more, Dusty simply sat rigid, eyes glued on the horrible phenomenon. As though by magic his sweat-drenched body went bone-dry. The skin of his face and hands grew taut under the make-up Curly had smeared over them. Then all of him became burning hot.

Then, a blasting, hissing sound. The interior of the cabin became a sea of flickering red. The control stick was wrenched from his grasp. Almost instantly it smashed back against his hands. But he hardly noticed the pain that shot up both arms to the shoulder sockets. The plane had slapped off the top of its zoom and he could just barely see Curly.

His pal sat as one dead; glassy eyes peered out from a pain-twisted face, stained the copperish glint of a Black Invader. Curly was staring unblinking out toward the left wing. His mouth was half open and lips quivered violently. It was as though he was trying to say something, but could not get sound out of a flame-seared throat.

Hardly conscious that he was moving, Dusty turned his head and looked toward the left, out the side cockpit window. His first impression was that the left wing-tip was cutting through a solid wall of fire. Then in a split second realization came to him.

The wall of fire was a long ways off, and streaking downward.

The reason that the wing-tip seemed to be cutting through the fire was because there was no wing-tip. Three feet of it had been mysteriously chewed off. No, not chewed off—melted off! The frayed, almost dripping edges of the wing covering curled up like wooden shavings right before his eyes.

Without warning he was suddenly slammed over against Curly's rigid body. The jolt seemed to start his brain clicking over. He realized that aileron control of the plane had become jammed and that the craft was falling over on one wing.

Brooks roared something in his ear, but he didn't hear what it was, nor did he bother to find out. Cursing savagely, he straightened up in the seat, got his feet and hands back on the controls, and tried desperately to bring the plane up onto an even keel.

He succeeded, almost. That is, by easing the stick back, and alternating the speed of the engines, he was able to get the plane up out of its mad dive toward the water. But it was impossible to hold it up. With sickening regularity, the craft slid off and down, first on one wing, and then on the other.

"If you can make it, the old tub should float for quite awhile!"

Curly's calm unhurried comment snapped Dusty back to complete possession of all his faculties. The very sound of his pal's voice was like a tonic. He jerked his head around, grinned into Curly's face that was now no longer twisted with pain and emotion.

"It'll be a long swim, if it doesn't float!" Dusty remarked.

Brooks returned the grin, said nothing, and stared out of the forward window. Battling the controls constantly Dusty took a second or two to look out the window himself.

The sky was no longer on fire, however, there was a dull red glow being thrown up from the rolling waters off to the left and in back of him. He didn't dare twist around to get a better look. He doubted if he could see anything, anyway.

With the fire gone from the sky, the shadows of early dawn were beginning to reappear. Of the strange craft he saw nothing. It had either flown away, or else was being blotted out from view by the reappearing shadows of early dawn.

"Just one ship! All the others were Yank crates! Good God—did you see any Black ships?"

Dusty shook his head, wrestled with the plane as it flip-flopped helplessly down toward the sea.

"No, didn't see a single one," he mumbled. "It was a trap. And we were almost caught in it!"

"Almost?" came Curly's harsh echo. "Hell, if this isn't the end, I'd like to know what is! But maybe one or two of them escaped and will pick us up. I don't get it, though! By God, I don't get it at all! What are those fire rings?"

Curly's words echoed the tantalizing thoughts racing around in Dusty's head. He didn't get it either. He felt like a man hopelessly lost in a jungle of mystery.

With a grating curse, Dusty shoved the disturbing thoughts to one side. This was no time to try to solve the mystery nor was it any use to attempt to discuss it with Curly. A safe landing on the rolling swells below was the paramount item at the moment.

He jerked his head toward Curly.

"Unhook the sealing lugs of the roof trap!" he snapped. "Get up on the seat and be ready to climb up through when we settle. But hold fast, we'll probably smack hard."

CURLY HESITATED, started to say something, but changed his mind. Instead he nodded abruptly, and getting up on the seat began to unhook the sealing lugs that held the cabin roof exit air-tight.

Meanwhile, fighting the sloppy movement of the craft every inch of the way, Dusty brought it down closer and closer to the water. A faint mist hung just over it, and although he was able to guess approximate wind direction, he was unable to do anything about an into-the-wind landing. With aileron control gone it was too risky to try and skid the plane around into the wind. It was going to be a cross-wind landing, or a crash.

The last hundred feet were made at almost stalling speed. Like a cripple being helped down a flight of stairs a step at a time, Dusty eased the bomber down those last hundred feet, a foot at a time.

Had it been a normal landing he might have noticed the wake of a submarine periscope in the water about three quarters of a mile away. But he didn't, and with face drawn and tensed, and every muscle of his body rigid, he stalled the bomber ten feet above the crest of a swell, and waited for it to settle.

For a fraction of a second the craft hung motionless, then, as though the invisible wires that suspended it had been cut, it sank down, tail first.

Instantly there was a terrific thump against the floor of the fuselage. And although Dusty had flung out both hands in the last split second and braced himself, he was thrown forward against the instrument board with battering-ram force. Only a lightning-like half twist of his body saved his face from being buried in the compass dial.

Dazed and badly shaken, he managed to wiggle back onto the seat and look up toward Curly. Brooks had the trap exit open and was hanging suspended on his crooked arms.

"You okay, Curly?"

"Yeah, guess so," came his pal's voice. "But you sure made good on the bump part. Sit tight while I get out, then I'll give you a hand."

The plane had settled by the nose, and water was beginning to seep in at the floor of the cabin. Pulling himself up onto the seat, Dusty braced himself against the angle and waited for Curly to wiggle up through the opening. That took but a minute, and as soon as Brooks' feet and legs disappeared his head and shoulders reappeared. He reached down with his right hand.

"Grab hold, Dusty. Watch your head as you come through."

Dusty obeyed, and in the matter of a few seconds, both he and Curly were sitting on the top of the cabin, their legs, from the knees down, dangling down through the trap exit.

In that way they were able to brace themselves against the motion of the half floating plane as it was heaved up and down by the rolling swells.

Curly fished in his tunic pocket, pulled his hands out empty, and cursed softly.

"Nuts! Left my smokes behind. You got any?"

Dusty fished with the same result. Curly sighed.

"Oh, well, been meaning to give them up for years," he muttered. "No time like the present." Then, casting his eyes out over the dim, gray water, "What do you think the chances are, Dusty?"

The other gazed out over the water, said nothing. There wasn't anything to say. That is, anything that might help. There was nothing to see but shifting shadows and shifting gray swells.

The red glow had completely disappeared. Clouds of smoke still hovered about high up in the sky. At least in the dim light of dawn they looked like clouds of smoke.

"That's what I think, too," Curly suddenly spoke again. "Old Dame Luck has given us the merry run around this time. But hell, if I only had a smoke!"

Dusty grinned, reached out and grabbed hold of Curly's arm.

"As usual, its my fault, Curly," he said. "I should never have let you come along. I'm sorry."

Brooks snorted.

"Your fault, my eye," he grated. "You couldn't have stopped me, and you know it. Oh, nuts, what's the sense of it all, anyway! We're here, and here we are. It's nice to have met you, Dusty, old kid. I've known worse guys—I guess."

Before Dusty could say anything, Brooks suddenly went rigid, half raised a hand and pointed ahead.

"Look—a periscope!" he gasped. "A sub, heading this way. God bless you, Lady Luck!"

It was true. As Dusty snapped his eyes around, he saw the curved top of a submarine periscope sliding through the water toward them. Instinctively he raised a hand and started waving wildly.

Oblivious to the rolling motion of the floating bomber he got up onto his feet and started waving both hands. Had not Curly wrapped both arms about his legs and held him, Dusty would undoubtedly have gone sliding off the top of the fuselage.

"They've spotted us!" Dusty shouted. "It's breaking surface. Hot dog, Curly, you'll get your smoke, now! You—"

Dusty stopped as the thought came to him. Both he and Curly were made up as a couple of Blacks, and they were on top of a Black bomber. If the approaching sub was a Yank navy boat they might be blown out of the water. After all that had happened, it was reasonable to believe that the Yanks would not take any chances—even with a couple of supposedly help-less pilots floating around in mid-ocean.

Heart pounding, Dusty stood motionless, watching the periscope come higher and higher out of the water. It was about fifty yards away, and moving through the water at a snail's pace—moving in a sort of half circle that would eventually bring it broadside to the floating plane.

Higher and higher the periscope came out of water. Then white foam splashed out to the sides and the top of the conning tower broke surface. Water spilled away from its gray-green sides.

A forward deck rapid fire anti-aircraft gun broke the surface, then the snub-nosed bow. The bow sank down under again as the craft was trimmed for surface running. And then like some great silent sea monster the entire top half of the submarine rose up clear of the water.

A shout died in Dusty's throat. His eyes, expecting to see the familiar U.S. navy submarine flotilla markings, saw no such thing. On the front of the conning tower was a white B with the number 26. And just under it, circled by a white band, was the conventional black flag of the Black Invaders!

CHAPTER 8
UNDERWATER PEELOTS

COUNTLESS CONFLICTING thoughts racing through Dusty's head, he watched the underwater craft sneak in close to the side of the plane. A moment or two later, the conning tower hatch swung open, and the head and shoulders of a Black naval officer appeared. In one hand he held a small megaphone. He raised it to his lips, and harsh Black Invader spoken words echoed across the water.

"Crawl out on the wing! The drift will bring us in close enough to take you off."

Dusty nodded his head, got down on his hands and knees, so that his head was close to Curly's.

"Get it, kid?" he whispered.

"Not all of it," came the answer. "Something about crawling on the wing? Hell, shall we?"

"We've got to!" Dusty hissed back. "We've got to—and pray like hell that we put it over. Play that you're hard of hearing,

Curly. Hit on the head when we landed. That way you'll be able to cover up anything you don't understand. Right! Here we go."

Twisting around, Dusty crawled along the top of the bobbing wing, and past the silenced engine. It was ticklish going. Swell spray made the metal covering as slippery as a greased plank. Half a dozen times he almost slid off into the water.

The sudden trembling of the wing made him look up. The submarine had drifted in close, and now three burly Black sailors were fending off the damaged tip of the wing. At the same time they were trying to hold the wing steady.

Dusty chanced a searching look at their faces. An expression of respectful curiosity was on each ugly face. A sense of hope flickered through him. He risked his voice as he got close.

"Take my hand," he snarled in their tongue. "Help me aboard, you blundering fools! Careful, now, curse you!"

Instantly one of the sailors released his grip on the wing, reached out and grabbed Dusty's left hand. Steadying himself, Dusty took two quick steps and a jump. The jump landed him on the water-soaked conning tower deck of the submarine. He immediately turned around and started to help Curly aboard. His help was not needed, however.

One of the other two sailors was already hoisting Curly aboard. Out of the corner of his eye Dusty saw the Black naval officer watching from the conning tower. It was a perfect chance to fix things for Curly.

"Careful with that officer!" he roared at the sailors. "He was injured when we landed. Struck his head. He has lost his hearing."

The sailors nodded, gave Curly a sympathetic glance. Then one of them pointed toward the conning tower hatch.

"The commander is waiting for you," he said. "We will get anything you have left."

Before Dusty realized what the man meant, the sailor had jumped onto the wing, and with the ease of a born acrobat trotted across its slippery surface to the trap exit in the cabin roof. Without bothering to shout that there was nothing worthwhile in the cabin Dusty turned and climbed the ladder to the conning tower hatch. Jet eyes bored into his as he reached a level with the Black naval officer.

"What happened? You are many miles from the *Teska!*"

Teska! Dusty wanted to shout for joy, but he didn't. So the bomber's carrier was the *Teska*, eh? Thank God the Black had told him instead of asking him. He shrugged, grimaced disgustedly.

"We were trapped in the raid on Washington," he said as his heart stood still in his chest. "The dog Americans almost surrounded us. We were driven far north. Then worse luck was ours. The left engine failed. We could barely keep in the air. An hour ago the skies exploded. Our left wing was damaged. We were helpless. We could do nothing but land!"

The Black made no move to step aside and let him climb down through the conning tower hatch. As a matter of fact he simply stood staring at him in annoyed amazement.

"The skies exploded?" he echoed gratingly. "Then you do not know what it was?"

Dusty's heart started down toward his boots. He knew that

he had made a mistake—had talked too much. The Black seemed dumbfounded that he didn't know what the sky phenomenon was.

A split second for thought, then he shrugged again and pushed his bluff act to the limit.

"No," he said. "We were only given orders to fly the course and return. Orders from Zytoff," he added as an afterthought.

The name Zytoff caused the hard gleam in the Black's eyes to abate somewhat. He mumbled something that Dusty didn't catch, stepped back.

"Come down below," he said gruffly. "There is brandy in the mess galley. You may want some. We can talk again, later."

A queer note in the man's voice sent little icy ripples sliding up and down Dusty's spine. There was nothing he could do, however, but obey.

Casting a glance downward to make sure that Curly was right at his heels, he swung first one leg and then the other over the lip of the conning tower opening and slid down onto the grilled steel platform at the head of a circular companionway ladder. The Black had already gone down the ladder to the control-room deck, and was waiting for him.

Hardly daring even to look at Curly, Dusty went down the ladder and followed the Black along a narrow companionway to a door at the far end.

When the Black shoved it open it proved to be the entrance to a small officers' mess. There were half a dozen chairs bolted to the floor along both sides of an oblong table, also fixed to the floor. Light was furnished by wall ports, and on the walls there were several framed photographs of Black submarines.

The Black paused at the doorway, nodded his head inside.

"Make yourselves comfortable," he said in what struck Dusty as a grudging tone. "I will have food and brandy sent you. And I will be back later."

AS THE man spoke, his eyes swung past Dusty to Curly. For perhaps five seconds they stared unblinking, and a strange glow smouldered in their depths. Then with a curt bow, the Black stepped away from the doorway and walked back toward the mid-section of the craft. Giving Curly the "come-on" nod, Dusty walked into the room and slumped down in one of the chairs. Curly, a troubled look in his eyes, sat down in a chair opposite him.

"I don't think we're going to get to first base! That mug smells something screwy!"

Curly's voice was even lower than a whisper. Dusty just barely heard him. He pulled down the corners of his mouth, and gestured significantly with his hands, fingers extended and palms facing upward. Then on sudden thought, he leaned forward.

"How is your head, now?" he asked loudly in Black Invader jargon. "Does it still pain?"

He winked and Curly took the cue instantly.

"What are you saying?" he asked in the same tongue. "You speak about our plane?"

Dusty grinned.

"No!" he shouted. "Not plane—pain! Does your head pain?"

"Yes, it is too bad about our plane!"

Just as Curly spoke the last a messboy entered the room carrying a tray. Sight of the food and bottle of brandy upon it sent Dusty's spirits soaring. There was nothing better than to meet trouble on a full stomach. And when he tried to, he couldn't recall just when he'd last eaten.

Without any comment he dived into the food placed before him. Curly was a close second for speed. For ten solid minutes they did nothing but eat. Then topping it off with a small brandy apiece they leaned back contentedly in their chairs.

Curly absently fished around in his pockets, but remembering that he didn't have any cigarettes, he issued a long unhappy sigh and fell to staring moodily at the pictures on the wall.

And it was about a minute after that, that the Black officer returned. He brought a second officer with him. A thin, cruel-faced man of junior rank. He carried a pad of paper and a pencil in his hand. Dusty must have stared at it questioningly, for the senior officer smiled, jabbed his thumb toward it.

"I will write my questions out for your friend, if he still cannot hear," he said. "And from your shouts just after I left you, I judge that he still has trouble. Now, will you please explain your experience to me again?"

Dusty tried to keep the strain he felt from showing in his face.

"Certainly," he said.

And then in unemotional, matter of fact tones he told a suitable chain of lies. At least he considered them suitable, and from the sympathetic nods that the Black gave him every now and then, he believed that the navy man considered them suitable also. The Black's first question, however, set his heart to pounding madly.

"There was not a third pilot with you?"

"Why no," Dusty replied shaking his head. "Just my comrade and myself."

A quiver ran through the boat, telling Dusty that they were getting underway. He looked at the Black officer. "Our destination?" he asked.

"I cannot tell you," came the curt reply. "We sail under secret orders. So there was no third person with you?"

"Why do you ask?"

The Black seemed not to hear Dusty's question. He turned and stared hard at Curly, particularly at his hands and face. Then he turned back and gave Dusty the same careful scrutiny. The queer puzzled glint had returned to his eyes.

"You say that your comrade, here, struck his head when you made your forced landing," he suddenly shot out. "It was not bad, that is obvious. Nor do you appear to be badly injured. Were you?"

DUSTY'S HEART skipped about six beats. He could feel sweat trickling down the back of his neck. And the palms of his hands became clammy. He knew that the Black was fishing for something, leading him on step by step. Though the man's manner was seemingly harmless, Dusty knew that a steel-trap brain was at work behind those jet black eyes that bored into his own. The man was playing him, yet not taking any chances of playing him too fast.

There was obviously only one answer to give the man.

"No, neither of us were hurt that badly," he said quietly. "And again I ask—why do you ask about a possible third comrade?"

"The blood," came the startling answer. "How do you account for it?"

"Blood?" Dusty got out thickly, and coming within an ace of saying it in English. "What about blood?"

"In the cabin of your plane," the Black replied, arching his eyebrows in evident surprise. "It is on the floor, and on the right wall. One of my crew noticed it—he told me about it. That is why I thought one of you was badly hurt."

With every ounce of his will power Dusty forced an expression of puzzled disbelief to remain on his face. But back of the temporary mask, memory was clicking over at lightning-like speed. Blood? Hell yes, he'd gun whipped that Black agent to a bleeding pulp. The man had splashed plenty around. In the dark, of course, he hadn't noticed. Or hadn't given it a thought, if he had noticed. But now—?

He let a knowing look flood into his face, threw back his head and laughed harshly.

"Ah yes!" he said. "Now I remember. I had forgotten all about that. The blood is from the nose of the pilot who usually flies with me. He is a clumsy fool at times. Yes, he was so eager for us to be off from the *Teska* that he ran his big nose against the cabin door jamb, as he entered. It was a good smash, and he bled like a stuck pig. I refused to let him come with me then. Besides, he needed a doctor's care. So my true comrade, here, came with me instead."

To Dusty's great relief the Black joined in the laugh.

"Ah, I understand, now," he said. "But, for a few moments, I was quite puzzled. You did not land on American territory, then?"

A silent note of warning shot through Dusty. He had the eerie feeling that he was in over his neck, and sinking deeper. A web of mystery was slowly closing in around him. But for the life of him he could not figure what it was about—what it was, that this Black was trying to find out.

"No, of course not," he said impulsively. "We would have been captured."

A tiny smile, or was it a smirk, tugged at the corners of the Black's mouth. He glanced at his junior officer, broadened his smile. Then he slowly swiveled his eyes around to Curly Brooks, and finally back to Dusty.

"That is strange," he murmured softly. "Very strange indeed. One of you, of course, is trying to be very clever, but you see, I have been told. I have been given my orders. Naturally I would not be in these waters, so close to the American forces—what is left of them—if it were not for you. Come, you can be honest with me. I know who you are."

Dusty could almost feel Curly go rigid. He knew that his pal had understood enough of the Black's words to get their general meaning. As for himself, every drop of blood in his veins seemed suddenly to freeze solid.

His was the feeling of a man who too late has realized that the supposedly solid earth beneath him is but quicksand. He stared into the Black's eyes, wondered if he could reach his holstered gun in time. The other smiled pleasantly.

"My deepest admiration, my comrade lieutenant," the Black said. "But you need not play the actor any more. I take back my question. I will no longer embarrass you. But to prove that I have been advised correctly, I will tell you who you are."

Time stood still. Dusty swallowed; didn't believe that he had spoken the words until they echoed back to him.

"And—who am I?"

The Black's eyes twinkled knowingly. He bobbed his head up and down like a small boy well pleased with himself for having ferreted out some secret he was not supposed to know. He even went so far as to shake a playful finger at Dusty.

"One of you—which, it does not matter—is Agent B Three-sixteen!"

As he finished the Black leaned back, gestured broadly and chuckled. Had a torpedo, or a depth bomb, caved in the side of the submarine at that moment, Dusty wouldn't have even noticed it. A surging wave of relief swept through him. Yet at the same time his body tingled with eerie foreboding. B Three-sixteen! The code number he had given to Zytoff over the radio! A code number he had made up in his own mind!

On impulse he had spoken that code number into the transmitter tube of a radio. Spoken it to Zytoff. And now, a Black submarine commander was calling him by that very same code number!

"You see, I have been advised! But you still wish to keep your little secret, eh? Very well, I admire you all the more for it. In fact, had you told me of your own accord I would have thought less of you. As we all know, it means death when one of our agents reveals his identity—when there is no occasion to do so."

Somehow Dusty managed to shrug. And somehow he managed to get the words out of his mouth that had gone bone dry.

"It is best for you to keep your secrets, and for us to keep ours."

"Very true, very true," the Black said parrot-like, and got to his feet. "Now I leave you to make yourselves comfortable. I am sorry, but I cannot permit you the freedom of my boat. As you say, we both have our little secrets. That button, there, on the wall—if you desire anything, press it."

The words came from Dusty's lips impulsively.

"Cigarettes," he said. "We left ours behind."

The naval officer dived into his pocket, pulled out a pack and matches, dropped them on the table.

"Allow me to give you mine," he smiled. "My own special brand. You will like them, I'm sure. And now, until we reach our destination—which, of course, you have already guessed—I leave you with my compliments."

And with stiff bows, the commander and his junior officer walked out of the mess cabin and closed the door behind them.

CHAPTER 9
FIRE-EYES

"**M**IND TELLING me the destination you're supposed to have guessed?"

Curly's whisper just barely carried across the table. Dusty swung his eyes back from the door through which the Blacks had passed, stared stupidly at his pal, and slowly shook his head.

"I haven't the faintest idea yet!"

"Yet?"

"Yeah, yet! Here, have one of these lung burners while I do some thinking. There's something beginning to percolate in the old bean—but I just can't put a finger on it. I'll nail it though, in a few minutes."

"Here's hoping!" murmured Curly, reaching for the cigarettes. "Damn this Black lingo anyway—I only got about one quarter of what he said. What about that B Three-sixteen stuff?"

"Shut up!" hissed Dusty. "I want to think!"

Slumping back in the chair, Dusty fixed half closed eyes on the opposite wall. And then, totally oblivious to the continued looks of puzzled annoyance that Curly shot toward him, he carefully retraced in his mind every single step he had taken since the very beginning of this cockeyed merry-go-round of mystery.

The minutes ticked by, became half an hour. Curly fidgeted in his chair, lighted his ninth cigarette in succession. He coughed meaningly a couple of times. But as far as Dusty was concerned, Curly was ten thousand miles away. An hour passed, and still

Dusty sat slumped in his chair like a man in a coma. The only movement was the occasional blinking of his eyelids.

Finally, though, he sat up straight, started to smash a clenched fist down on the table but caught himself in time.

"Got it, Curly!" he breathed fiercely but softly. "By God, I believe I've got it!"

Curly grimaced, snubbed out his cigarette.

"About time you got something. Me, I've got the jitters! Well?"

Dusty leaned forward so that his head was but a bare two or three inches from Curly's.

"The Black agent who killed the Washington field radio sergeant!" he whispered rapidly. "His job must have been to keep on General Horner's tail. Either that, or he was to dig up something important in Washington and communicate that knowledge to Fire-Eyes.

"Naturally, Fire-Eyes would not risk taking it direct. So, his pet favorite, Zytoff, was the go-between. Something went haywire, so Zytoff instead of taking my report over the air—perhaps because I said that the Yanks had learned the code—ordered me, thinking I was the agent, to the AT-Twenty-two area, where this submarine would pick me up!"

"Maybe," nodded Curly, as Dusty paused for breath. "But how did Zytoff know that this Washington agent was going to be in a plane?"

"No, you don't get the idea," Dusty frowned. "Listen, you didn't have much trouble, you and Biff, forcing that bomber down—it wasn't with the others, was it?"

"No, it wasn't. All by itself, about ten miles up the coast. The rest were way south, milling with our coastal planes."

"There's the answer, Curly! Listen, this agent—that I'm supposed to be—was after something hot in Washington. What, damned if I can even guess. However, in case he couldn't get word through via radio, he was to be picked up by the bomber you and Biff forced down.

"By luck, you and Biff came down the coast and bumped into the bomber. That made the agent out of luck. So he tears back for Washington, hoping that he can get word through that he missed the ship that was to pick him up.

"Anyway, he tried to get word through via the Washington field radio station. The sergeant scared him away, so what does he do? The only thing he can do—hides himself in the plane he's supposed to be in, anyway.

"Luckily, I trip him up—and pinch-hit on the radio. And Zytoff, thinking that he's in the plane that picked him up, gives me orders to go to the place where I'll be met by this submarine. In other words, it had been planned for that bomber to meet this submarine. And, instead, we've met it!"

"It sounds logical," murmured Curly, frowning. "But where do we go from here?"

Dusty reached out his hand, took hold of Curly's arm.

"We go," he said in a hushed voice, "to where it was originally planned for that Black agent to go. To wherever Fire-Eyes is—to make the report in person!"

Curly's eyes became saucers, and he swallowed three times in rapid succession.

"My God!" he gasped, "you think of the happiest endings!"

Dusty shrugged.

"I may be wrong," he said. "May be screwy as hell. But damned if that isn't the way it shapes up to me. There's only one thing that bothers me."

"Only one thing?"

"Yeah!" Dusty whispered. "B Three-sixteen! I thought that code number up on the spur of the moment. There isn't a chance in a billion that I could have hit on the exact code number of that Black agent.

"It's just possible, though, that Zytoff didn't know the real code number. He only knew, probably, that it was the right man because of the wave-length reading that I contacted him on. The agent set it, you see. And ten to one, it was the registered reading for that bomber."

"But this wall-eyed sub commander knew it!" breathed Curly.

Dusty scowled at the top of the table a minute, before answering. Suddenly, his face lighted up in a smile.

"PART OF my guessing was wrong," he said. "Where we met this sub was not the original meeting place. That's why the commander told me that I was a long ways from the *Teska*. Zytoff probably told him that he had given B Three-sixteen orders to go to AT-Twenty-two and be picked up."

Curly squinted his eyes in heavy thought for a moment or two. Then he heaved a long, dubious sigh.

"Everything you say seems to check," he murmured, "except one thing."

"Yeah?"

CURLY BROOKS

"Yeah! B Three-sixteen has valuable information. Yet—Zytoff orders him to proceed to a spot where he may run the risk of being wiped out. And what's more—damn near was wiped out! That, my friend, doesn't make sense to this aged head."

Curly's brutal but unquestionably sane logic sent Dusty's spirits whizzing down the skids. He nodded his agreement absently, furrowed his brows and tried to think of a suitable answer. There just wasn't any, however. No matter at what angle he regarded it, he met the same solid wall of cold reasons—if B Three-sixteen had valuable information, Zytoff certainly wouldn't order him to his death. That sort of thing just wasn't being done, even among the Blacks.

Taking a cigarette, Dusty lighted up. He took one puff and hurled it to the floor in disgust. Curly must have lungs of plated steel to smoke those things. Getting to his feet he began to wander musingly around the mess cabin. When he passed the door he stopped, and impulsively tried the knob. It wouldn't turn. The door was securely locked on the other side. Curly grinned crookedly as their eyes met.

"Think a way out of this one, B Three-sixteen!" he grunted.

Dusty gave him the agate eye, walked back to his chair and slumped down into it. For the want of something better to do, he glanced at his wrist watch. To his amazement he saw that it was close to noon. It didn't seem possible. He put the watch to his ear, realized that it was ticking smoothly. So it was true—almost ten hours had passed since he and Curly left the Washington field.

At that moment an invisible force thrust him back in the

chair, and it thrust Curly up against the edge of the table. For a couple of seconds Dusty thought that the submarine had been hit. Then he realized what was taking place. The sub was breaking surface after an underwater run. He glanced at Curly, saw the question in his eyes that he was asking himself. Had they reached their destination?

Almost automatically, he pulled his gun from its holster, and inspected it closely. It was in good working order. Sticking it back, he glanced toward his pal, again.

"Up to Lady Luck, now," he grunted softly. "But if it's ixnay, get all you can while you can—maybe him, if we meet him."

"Right through one of those damn blazing eyes of his!" Curly grated back. "And I hope to God that I get just one chance!"

Dusty nodded, but made no reply. A feeling of utter hopelessness was stealing over him again. He tried to beat it off, but it stayed with him.

For hours both he and Curly had been living on borrowed time. He could feel it in his bones. All the luck in the world had been theirs. But was it going to get them anything? Was it going to last? For a thousand years, it seemed, he had been groping about in the dark—for just one tiny thread of light to guide him to a definite goal. And he was still groping!

There was a clicking sound in the door lock. It swung open, and the submarine commander stepped inside. He was smiling pleasantly, almost joyously. Like a cat who has swallowed the canary, it struck Dusty.

"We have arrived, my comrades," he smiled. "If you will come with me."

Dusty got slowly to his feet, then almost groaned aloud as he realized that Curly was already on his feet and walking toward the door. Curly, who was supposed to have lost his hearing! Too late, Curly realized his blunder. The submarine commander gave him a shrewd, calculating look.

"Ah, then it is not permanent, eh?" he murmured. "You are able to hear?"

Dusty held his breath. Curly leaned forward, like a man trying to hear every word.

"My hearing?" he said falteringly, in the Black native's tongue. "Yes, I can hear a little."

It was all Dusty could do to stop himself from leaping across the mess cabin and slapping his pal on the back. Curly had understood enough of what the Black had said to get the meaning, and his accent when he replied had been well-nigh perfect. It certainly seemed to meet with the approval of the submarine commander too. He smiled, and bowed.

"I'm very glad. I was worried. We have no doctor aboard, and there was nothing I could do to help you. Now, this way, my comrades."

For a split second the eyes of the two Yanks met, and read the other's reflected thought—thank God, there hadn't been a doctor aboard the submarine!

Leading the way, the commander stepped out into the companionway and started toward the conning tower deck. Dusty hesitated, but killed a wild hope that had suddenly sprung up within him, as he saw the armed sailor waiting respectfully for them to follow the Black officer. Giving the man a hard look he stepped through the door and made his way along the companionway, with Curly right at his heels.

Instead of going up the conning tower ladder, the Black made his way forward and pushed open a small bulkhead door. Dusty followed, and found himself on the forward deck near the rapid-fire antiaircraft gun. The gun didn't interest him, however.

The thing that nailed his complete attention immediately was the massive armor-plated hulk about a hundred yards off the port bow. In other words, the Black airplane carrier riding low down in the water.

IN SPITE of the ticklishness of his present situation, Dusty could not help but stare in unconcealed admiration at the carrier. It was of the latest type; a craft of speed, formidableness, and efficiency from bow to stern.

It sat well down in the water to counteract excess rolling during plane maneuvers in heavy weather. Its flight deck was clear of any obstruction, the two funnels, and navigating bridge being set at an angle on the port side that more or less brought them out over clear water.

The aft part of the flight deck was covered with planes in take-off formation position. Planes of all types, but none with props ticking over. Below the flight deck eight-and twelve-inch-gun turrets were visible, concrete evidence that the craft could hold its own in any kind of a sea engagement.

"This way, my comrades. The tender will take you over to her."

The Black's voice snapped Dusty back to the present. Nosed in close to the port rail of the submarine was a small Diesel-powered tender. She was manned by a couple of Black sailors and a junior naval flight officer. The submarine commander was pointing at it.

Dusty smiled, snapped the Black Invader salute, then grabbed hold of the chain rail of the submarine and leaped lightly down into the tender cockpit. Curly Brooks jumped down after him.

Instantly the tender shoved over, swung her nose around, and started gliding through the rolling blue green swells toward the carrier. She hoved to on the starboard side, and the crew made her fast to the gangway ladder. The junior officer stepped up on to the platform, motioned to Dusty and Curly.

"You will follow me, please," he said.

There wasn't much else they could do. And so, each with his own troubled thoughts the two Yanks went up the gangway ladder to a port entrance just under the flight deck. There they were met by two officers of commanders rank. The junior flight officer saluted and disappeared. The two ranking ones fixed piercing black eyes on Dusty and Curly.

"Your code number?" one of them suddenly snapped.

Dusty took the bit in his teeth.

"B Three-sixteen," he said. Then nodding toward Curly, "My good comrade and I have been working together."

"I see," replied the Black in a tone that made Dusty's blood go down below the freezing point. "Well, your work together has finished. You, B Three-Sixteen, will come with me. Your comrade will go with this other officer."

Dusty hesitated. Of all things, he didn't want to be separated from Curly.

"And may I ask why?" he got out harshly. "Are we to consider ourselves as prisoners, who have done some wrong?"

He put scorn into the last, and steeled himself inwardly. The sensation of eerie foreboding was sweeping over him again. To his relief the Black officer looked surprised.

"Prisoners?" he echoed. "Hardly! But B Three-sixteen knows that he has information for the ears of only one man. Come! We have lingered here long enough. You can join your good comrade later."

Dusty looked at Curly, forced a hopeful grin to his lips.

"Be of good cheer," he said slowly in the Black Invader tongue. "The separation will be only temporary."

Though it was the flowery type of conversation between Black Invader friends, Dusty prayed fervently that Curly would get the underlying meaning. In other words—"Chin up, kid! We'll still be able to draw more cards!"

Curly smiled back, sucked in his breath.

"I shall wait content," he said, with perfect accent.

Turning back to the officer who had addressed him, Dusty nodded and motioned with his hand for the other to lead the way. The journey consisted of going aft to a point slightly aft of 'midships, then down grilled companionway ladders to the waterline deck, and aft some more until finally the Black stopped before a cabin door.

He lifted his hand and jabbed a button studded in the jamb. A couple of seconds later a tiny white light at top of the door glowed into life, and there was clicking sound in the lock.

Instantly the Black grasped the door knob, pushed the door open and stepped back as he did so.

"You will enter," he said.

Dusty stepped into a room flooded with brilliant light. It blinded him momentarily. He blinked rapidly, tried to focus his eyes. He heard the door click shut behind him. Then his eyes became adjusted to the glare, and he glanced around.

He found himself in a high-ceilinged square room. There were chairs, very comfortable looking ones, too. And tables covered with charts and books. A thick rug was on the floor. Bookcases, and countless charts lined the side walls.

In one corner there was a huge ten-foot globe, virtually covered with little colored flag pins. At the far end of the room, directly opposite him, there was a small dais. A massive carved wood chair stood on the dais. And in the chair sat a figure, the very sight of whom straightened Dusty's backbone stiff as a ramrod, and made his heart thump savagely against his ribs.

The figure seated in the chair was Fire-Eyes, supreme commander of the Black Invaders, and self-styled Emperor of the World!

CHAPTER 10
YANK LIGHTNING

FOR PERHAPS two full seconds, Dusty stared into the slitted, blazing orbs that virtually burned out at him from behind the stiff green mask. Then he snapped his right hand up in the conventional Black Invader salute—fingers extended upward, on a level with the right shoulder, and the palm facing forward. And as he saluted, he shouted the Black Invader chant of homage to their supreme leader.

"He-e-e la-a-a zo!"

That all done with he stood waiting, heart skipping beat after beat, and a crazy, mixed-up conglomeration of thoughts racing madly around inside his brain.

Presently, an eternity to Dusty, and the black-garbed, green masked figure, moved. He inclined his head slightly. Then like the roll of distant thunder words came from behind the green mask.

"You come to me with news?"

"I come to the Supreme One with news," Dusty stalled. Then as he thought quickly, "I come with much news. What news does the Supreme One desire first?"

A moment of silence, during which the blazing orbs seemed almost to burn holes in Dusty's face. It was all he could do to keep himself from turning his head and looking anywhere but at that green mask.

"Your secret code number is what?"

"My secret code number is B Three-sixteen, Supreme One," Dusty answered.

Silence again. A heavy stifling silence that made sweat ooze out at the nape of Dusty's neck and go trickling down his backbone. For a crazy instant he was seized with a mad desire to go for his automatic and place a hunk of steel through one of the two slits in the green mask.

But several sane reasons killed the idea. The range was too

risky, even for his marksmanship. Also, if he could but find out what information Fire-Eyes desired it might give him an inkling as to where, when, and how the Black Invaders intended to launch their next blow—if it had not already been launched.

And another reason, a mighty important one, incidentally, it was an odds-on bet that other eyes besides those of the supreme commander were watching him. Something, call it a sixth sense, told him that he and Fire-Eyes were not alone. Let him but make a move for his gun and he'd go out like a light.

No, better to let his gun alone for the present. Fire-Eyes wore bullet-proof clothing. He knew that from past experience. The man's only vulnerable spots were those two blazing orbs behind the slits in the green mask. And, hell, the range wasn't worth a try, yet.

"So your code number is B Three-sixteen?"

The words boomed out, seemed to literally smack Dusty in the face. He sensed the beginning of the end, but he doggedly stuck to his guns.

"That is the code number I have used, Supreme One," he replied evenly.

"I do not believe you," the green mask thundered back. "However, I shall give you a chance to prove yourself. What do the dog Americans know of my whereabouts? Where do they believe me to be? And where do they expect me to strike? Answer me those questions, and I shall know whether to believe you or not."

Dusty's brain raced over at top speed. Should he bluff or tell the truth? That is, tell the truth insofar as he knew it?

"Well, why do you hesitate?"

"Only to choose my words, Supreme One," Dusty said humbly. "I wish to collect all the facts I have learned in the American capital. Supreme One, they believe that you are on your way to Bermuda. And they believe that you will attack their eastern coast with a large naval and air force. They do not, however, know how their Atlanta concentration base, and their munitions depot at Roanoke were destroyed. You have completely fooled them, Supreme One."

A noise like high explosives going through the walls crashed about the room. Dusty ducked instinctively, but realized a split second later that the sound was but roaring laughter coming from behind the green mask.

"They believe I go to Bermuda, huh? When, B Three-sixteen? Tell me when?"

The emphasis on the last word was akin to a knife going through Dusty's heart. There was a dreaded, ominous ring to it that made him seem to shrivel up inside. Just why, he couldn't say. In some crazy way he felt that it was a catch question. In fact, he knew it, just as sure as he knew the sun rose in the east and set in the west. Yet, for the life of him he didn't know how it should be answered.

"I do not exactly understand the Supreme One's question," he stalled desperately for time.

"It is a simple enough question, you fool!" came back the bellowing words. "Yesterday, today, tomorrow, next week—when do they expect me to go to Bermuda?"

Dusty took a chance.

"Last night they believed you to be on your way."

Silence, heavy and sinister. Dusty knew that he had said the wrong thing. Face blank, eyes riveted on the slitted green mask, he moved his right hand a fraction of an inch nearer his holstered gun. But, no more than that.

"So!" the words seemed to virtually burst up through the steel plated ceiling. "So, I was on my way last night, hah? Then, some one was caught. Some one was caught, and that information forced from his lips. You were working alone, B Three-sixteen?"

"I was working alone, Supreme One."

"And you do not know of any of your comrades being caught? One of my airplane pilots, perhaps?"

Dusty shook his head.

"I know of no one being caught, Supreme One."

More torturing silence. Then suddenly, Fire-Eyes shot out his long right arm, grabbed a cord, that Dusty noticed for the first time, and jerked on it once. Almost instantly a section of the bookcases on Dusty's left swung open, and a tall, good-looking man in the uniform of a Black Invader air force pilot officer stepped into the room. Dusty didn't have to look at him twice. He recognized the man instantly.

None other than Zytoff, of course.

The Black ace saluted his senior, and stood at respectful attention. Fire-Eyes did not even turn his head. He swung up his right gauntleted hand, pointed the big forefinger at Dusty.

"You will question him, and I will listen!" he boomed. "The

part on which I have just touched is the part of which you had charge. Proceed!"

Zytoff nodded, turned and took a couple of steps toward Dusty. Although he was not sure the Yank thought he saw a tiny grin tugging at the corners of the Black ace's mouth. Then the man spoke.

"You will please give me your report now! The report I refused over the radio."

Dusty tried a long shot.

"It is of no use now," he said. "I wished to inform you of American navy movements toward northern waters."

"And that is all?"

"What else did you desire, my comrade officer?" asked Dusty, fighting to keep surprise in his voice. "Did you not wish to know that, because of the Supreme One's movements?"

NO SOONER had Dusty got the words out of his mouth, than he knew that his blind random shot had smacked the nail right smack on the head. Zytoff nodded his head, and a faintly puzzled look came into his eyes.

"That is true," he said. Then after a short pause, "But that was not all I expected. What about information regarding the reorganizing of American air defense bases along their eastern coast?

"Did you not send out the radio order to draw all their air units up to the Central Atlantic states? You were to inform us when that had been accomplished!"

Zytoff cut himself off short, leaned forward. The smouldering death in his eyes.

"That radio message was not sent?" he barked.

Dusty's brain pounded like a dynamo gone haywire. Draw all Yank air units up to the Central Atlantic states? Had the murderer of the Washington field radio sergeant sent out a message after all? Had he sent out a fake concentration message to all available air units? If so, for God's sake, why?

If the Blacks were going to launch a smashing sea and air attack against the east coast, why try to get American forces concentrated there to meet them? True, Atlanta and Roanoke were gone. That left the southeastern area crippled. But the Yanks could still rally plenty of resistance against a Central Atlantic states attack.

"Are you deaf, fool? Or does your silence mean that you have failed? Did you send that message?"

"Yes, of course I sent it, my comrade officer," Dusty lied. "And may I ask—when does the attack begin? For my services, I should like to be with the advance attack."

Zytoff ignored the question. He half turned and faced Fire-Eyes. Then words rushed off his lips so fast that Dusty was unable to get but a couple of them here and there. He heard the words—"lie, do not believe them, and advise we delay attack until sure." The Black commander nodded his head slowly, and once more Dusty actually felt the burning heat of his horrible eyes. Suddenly words boomed out from behind the green mask.

"You toy with death, B Three-sixteen. I give you one more chance. There is one bit of information you have not given to me. It is the most important of all. Have the Tenth, Thirtieth, and Forty-first American super-cruiser and aircraft battle squadrons changed their positions? Tell me the truth and you will be rewarded beyond your highest hopes!"

Dusty felt as though the floor was slipping away from beneath his feet. He wished with all his heart that Curly was with him. Curly could answer that question, for only a week ago he had acted as special navy air force courier attached to the aircraft carrier *Stamford*.

The *Stamford* was one of the ships in the Forty-first aircraft battle squadron. Curly would know where they were, and could give some dizzy answer. But he didn't. For all he knew the three squadrons might be plowing through the ice at the North Pole.

Hell, and double hell. If he'd only taken the trouble to ask Curly when he was relieved of courier duty. But he hadn't. He'd been too busy studying the damn Black Invader lingo. And Curly hadn't made any mention of it, for the reason that courier work was so damn boring that you promptly forgot about it when your assignment was over.

But Fire-Eyes wanted an answer. Dusty knew from the way the big man leaned forward that the information would be of vital importance to him. He sucked in his breath sharply, and staked his fate on a bluff answer.

"The squadrons of which you speak, Supreme One," he said slowly, "are still at their same positions off the New England coast."

Zytoff cursed harshly. Then he suddenly broke into a wild laugh. He took three quick steps toward Dusty, stopped and stood regarding him through narrowed lids.

"American dog," he barked out in English, "your fool's game

has now come to an end. You have told us what we want to know. Prepare to die!"

Dusty forced a half-puzzled, half-injured look to his face.

"My comrade officer speaks insulting words when he calls me an American dog."

"Silence, you fool! We have had enough. You are a fool, and so is your superior officer, General Horner, for selecting so stupid a man for such a delicate task. B Three-sixteen? Bah! There is no B Three-sixteen! But had you guessed the correct code number, we would still have known."

Dusty sparred desperately for time so that he might inch his hand back a bit more toward his holstered gun. He knew that he was trapped and sunk—that the next few minutes meant his life.

"But my comrade officer!" he shouted, still speaking in the language of the Black Invaders.

"Enough! Hold your lying tongue. Do you think that one of our agents in Washington would wear the uniform that you now wear? Do you think that one of our agents in Washington would have a skin so dark as yours? You fool, some day when I meet your superior, General Horner, I shall tell him how he neglected to advise you to leave your American-made wrist watch at home!"

THE STRAP holding Dusty's watch seemed to burn into the skin of his wrist as Zytoff snarled out the damning words. Like a collapsing house of cards everything he had accomplished as an American agent went flat as a stove cover. He wanted to boot himself into eternity for his colossal stupidity.

My God, yes, the murderer of the Yank radio sergeant had looked like an American, of course! Worn an American uniform,

SOMETHING SMACKED AGAINST HIS GUN HAND

too. And all this time he'd thought he was getting away with an impersonation of that man, when in reality he was all made up as the blackest of Black Invaders.

He felt sure that he had fooled only himself ever since he and Curly had dropped down into the water. The submarine commander had been wise. So had Fire-Eyes, and so had Zytoff. But they had let him continue to play his dumb game.

Why? Because they wanted the information that the real agent could probably give them. They had asked him all kinds of trick questions. Questions that seemed stupid to him. Yet— and his heart chilled at the thought—in trying to match his cleverness with theirs, had he accidentally told them part of what they wanted to know?

The voice of Fire-Eyes crashed in on his swirling thoughts.

"There are several ways to kill a dog. You can shoot him, and get it over quickly. You can chain him to the floor and let rats eat their fill of his flesh. You can apply the ancient water death, a drop at a time on his forehead until he goes permanently insane.

"Or you can have a drop of acid instead of water—a drop of acid on each joint in the body, and two for each eye. The ways to kill a dog are many. What if I gave you your choice?"

The Black commander spoke in perfect English. But, as Dusty replied, he still stuck to the Invader lingo. One tiny consoling thought was his. They did not know who he was. At least he was concealing his true identity. And by God, that was one satisfaction he'd keep from them to the very end.

"What does it matter which I choose?" he flung back. "Death is death, in the end!"

"True!" came back the booming voice. "But there can be much horrible pain and suffering before the end. Answer a question I shall ask you, and I promise a swift end. Death will be yours, but there will be no pain—no pain that you will remember long after you are dead!"

"Ask the question, and I will decide if I shall answer it!" Dusty hurled at him.

"Very well then. The question I asked a few moments ago—have the Tenth, Thirtieth and Forty-first squadrons changed their positions? Do not lie. As a dog American agent, that is one thing you would be bound to know. Now tell me."

"And if I tell you, on my word, that I do not know?" Dusty countered, and steeled himself as he felt his right hand press against his gun.

The answer came back to him instantly.

"I would know that your word was a lie! You know, and you can tell me. Remember my bargain. Speak!"

Dusty let his shoulders droop, as though he was giving up in complete surrender. But the movement enabled him to shift the weight of his body onto the left foot. And it also drew back his right arm. He looked straight at Fire-Eyes, but out of the corner of his eye he could see Zytoff. The Black ace was leaning forward, body rigid, and his right hand a good six inches from his gun.

"A swift death, then," said Dusty. "I'll tell you. The Tenth, Thirtieth, and Forty-first aircraft battle squadron have been moved—to—"

The Yank paused, went through the facial motions of a broken man fighting desperately to keep up his courage.

"Moved to where?" came the roaring question.

Dusty gulped like a fish out of water.

"Moved—to—"

Lightning! That's the only way to describe Dusty's movements as he pivoted, dropped into a half crouch, and jerked his gun free. But even at that, they were not fast enough.

Before his finger had curled about the trigger, the walls crashed out sound. Something smacked against his gun hand, shot white fire clear up his arm to the shoulder socket. Something hot and hissing streaked across his right cheek. The room became bathed in red haze.

He saw Zytoff clutch at his chest, cry out sharply and drop to the floor in a heap. There came a bellowing roar from Fire-Eyes. The Black commander was halfway out of his chair. He turned to the left, stumbled down off the dais, and went charging toward the left side of the room.

Dully, Dusty was conscious that he was flat on his back on the floor. Through glassy eyes he saw his gun four feet away from his bleeding right hand. He tried frantically to force his body toward it, but the ceiling fell down on his face in a terrific crash.

CHAPTER 11
CHECKMATE

NEEDLES—THOUSANDS OF them, white with heat, pricking every square inch of skin on his body. They passed clear through him, came out the opposite side, and then cut back in again.

"Damn you to hell! I won't tell you a thing! I won't tell you a damn thing! Curse the whole lot of you—curse you to hell and back!"

The sound of his own voice echoing back through his half stunned senses, pried Dusty's eyelids open. At first he could see absolutely nothing. A billion shadows were swimming around in a sea of glaring light.

In an abstract sort of way he knew that he was lying on his side, on something hard. The glaring light hurt his eyes. He closed them, and tried desperately to rally his strength. From head to foot there was no feeling in his body. His brain commanded his legs to move, but he could not feel them move. A thousand tons of lead seemed to be pressing down on every muscle of his body.

He opened his eyes to narrowed slits. Shadows were still swimming about. But they were going slower, now, much slower. He sucked air into his hot and aching lungs. At first he thought he was going to faint. Everything started racing madly around inside his head.

Then his brain cleared, and he found himself looking along the surface of a thick rug. A couple of seconds later familiar objects presented themselves clearly. Chairs, tables, charts, bookcases, and a huge globe. It was then that he realized he was still in the same room.

For a couple of moments he blinked stupidly. Then tried to get up. But he couldn't—couldn't move a single muscle. Sweat poured off his face. The needles started piercing his body again, yet the pain of them was little more than a dull ache.

Suddenly he realized that he could move his head. It seemed to fly off his shoulders as he moved it. But he gritted his teeth and mushed his right cheek through the rug nap until he could see his legs. Every part of him screamed aloud for those legs to move, but like lead pipes they remained motionless, one flung grotesquely across the other.

"My God—I'm paralyzed—I'm paralyzed!"

He shouted the words aloud in sudden panic. Then with sweat streaming from his face he cursed himself to move; his legs to move, and his arms. Finally, though, he lay gasping for breath, as the horrible truth seared a path across his brain. From the neck down he was completely paralyzed.

"It must be fate, for things to end this way, Captain Ayres!"

A voice! Zytoff's voice!

For a moment, Dusty burst out with insane laughter. Then he cut it off short, forced his splitting head back. He could just barely see the crumpled form about ten feet away. Zytoff was lying on his stomach, head twisted to the left, one arm flung out on the rug, and the other crooked under him. The side of the man's neck nearest Dusty was red with blood. Blood was also seeping through the nap of the rug from under the left side of the man's chest.

As Dusty looked at him, the Black's lips quivered, twitched back in a twisted grin.

"Ten feet, and yet neither of us can reach that gun! It is fate, my friend. Fate that we should die together, yet so many, many worlds apart."

Dusty saw the gun. It was his own. On the rug, ten feet from his outflung paralyzed arm. He swiveled his eyes back to Zytoff, grinned.

"Yeah, tough!" he said. "I'm sorry, Zytoff—that I didn't get you clean. I don't like to see even a Black die this way."

"You didn't fire your gun, captain," came the choking words. "You didn't fire a single shot. It was—someone else. The one who was with you. Who was he—Lieutenant Horner? He's a fool, if he thinks he has helped any."

CURLY! CURLY Brooks! His pal's name crashed through Dusty's brain. Had Curly fired some of those shots? But that was impossible! How could Curly have found the room? How could he have fired any of those shots? No, it couldn't have been Curly.

He stared at Zytoff, moved his head in a negative motion the fraction of an inch.

"One of your own gang, Zytoff, if it wasn't me. You Blacks were always rotten shots. Had them park behind the walls, eh? I had a feeling they were there."

"Yes, they were there, Ayres. You see, we knew that you were no agent of ours. It was too crude. But I'll tell you something, my friend—let us call it a farewell compliment—I did not know that it was you, until I heard you cry out in your own native tongue a few moments ago. You at least fooled us that much."

The Black's words grew weaker and weaker as he talked. They seemed to come out of his mouth like drops of water from a leaking bucket.

"Thanks," Dusty grunted. Then, suddenly, "How about Roanoke, Zytoff?"

Zytoff had closed his eyes, but his lips twitched into a smile. A tremor ran through his limp body. It was almost as though the man were chuckling to himself.

"Something you'll never know, my friend. Something that will spell complete victory for us. Fate has decreed that I shall not live to see that victory. But I'm only one man. And I die content, captain. Die, knowing that we shall ultimately crush you into obedient submission.

"This time, nothing can save your country. The Supreme One's plans have been well thought out. And everything, even to the minutest detail, has been well done. Your—country is—doomed to defeat!"

The eyelids fluttered closed, and the Black lay so perfectly limp and motionless that Dusty was positive he had died. A great conglomeration of mixed emotions sweeping through him, he stared silently at a man, who, though a hated enemy of the United States, was nevertheless a man of great daring and courage, and complete devotion and loyalty to duty.

But Zytoff had not died yet. Dusty saw his lips move back in a smile again, heard the huskily spoken words that came out from between them.

"It is kismet, yes! Or checkmate, if you wish. You fooled me, and I fooled you. That radio order I gave you, captain—to go to AT-Twenty-two. I knew you were not the right agent. But—I did not know it was you."

The Black coughed, sprayed blood. Dully Dusty wondered why he did not die. It seemed unbelievable that there was a single drop of blood left in the man's veins. But Zytoff went on speaking.

"That was your mistake, captain—to go to AT-Twenty-two. Had you been the real agent, you would have gone elsewhere. Luck was yours, however—luck and the fact that I was too busy destroying the American planes and battleships to take care of you until it was too late.

"You managed to get down into the water. One of our submarines picked you up—one that I had ordered to that area on the chance that you were not the agent bringing us information. When you were picked up—I could not radio the submarine commender. I had static-jammed the entire area. But he had received previous orders. He brought you here—I came here. And it is kismet. You have not found out what you wanted to know. We have not—yet—found out what we wanted to know. But that—is only a question of time."

Zytoff's voice trailed off again. Dusty continued to stare at him, and silently battled with his thoughts.

"Zytoff!" he suddenly called out. "Fire-Eyes' going to Bermuda—it was a bluff, eh?"

"It was a bluff that worked perfectly," came the almost whispered reply. "As your navy will find out, too late. That—was your final blunder, captain. A blunder to say that the Americans knew that the Supreme One had left. Every one of our pilots was told that—told it in case he was captured and forced to talk. When you spoke I knew that one of our bombers had been forced down—the bomber you flew to AT-Twenty-two. No agent would have said that—for none of our agents knew.

"But the goal has been gained. Your ships and your aircraft will rush to those cursed islands—and find nothing. And before they can return—ah-h-h, it will be much too late then!"

The faint note of triumph in the man's words rasped Dusty to the core.

"You're wrong, Zytoff!" he snapped. "Wrong as hell! Bermuda is one spot where all aircraft and surface ships have been ordered to stay away from!"

The Black's eyes flew open wide, flooded with a glazed look of mad disbelief.

"No!" he choked. "You lie! You lie, dog! There is nothing your leaders want more than to capture the Supreme One. Their desires fitted into his plans. He was the bait that drew them away from our true objective."

Dusty laughed. Then suddenly cut it off with a choking gasp. A strange tingling sensation was rippling through his right foot. Teeth clenched against the pain, he twisted his head down, and looked. Glory be to God—he could move his foot!

FROM A long way off he heard Zytoff's whispering voice again. But he didn't pay any attention. The tingling sensation was rippling up the calf of his right leg to the knee. It had also crept into his left foot. He wasn't paralyzed after all. He wasn't going to have to lay there helpless until some of the Blacks came back to finish him for good! Life was coming back into the lower part of his body.

He wanted to cry out—shout the news at the top of his voice. Hope, that he had subconsciously abandoned, returned to him in a seething turmoil of emotion. He must get out of this damn room before any of the others came back. He must find Curly. Curly! God alone knew what had happened to him by now. Was he dead? Had he fired those shots? Where was Fire-Eyes? He'd stumbled when he'd leaped down off that dais! Stumbled like a man winged by a bullet!

Dusty lived through the torture of the damned as life slowly seeped back into his paralyzed body. How he had been paralyzed, he could only guess. The back of his neck smarted horribly. A bullet had probably glanced off a nerve center. But the hell with wondering how he had been paralyzed! Movement was coming back to him. He could move both of his legs, from the hips down! And yes—there—those wiggling fingers that he was staring at were attached to his right hand.

Dusty was now able to get up on his hands and knees. He shut his eyes tight, fought desperately against a crazy swaying motion that was trying to sway him out over the lip off a yawning pit of utter darkness. Gradually the swaying sensation left him. He felt the fingers of both hands curling into the thick nap of the rug. The back of his right hand was on fire. But pain—even the terrible pain at the base of his skull didn't bother him now. The overwhelming joy at being able to move again blotted out everything else.

"So it is not fate, after all! Just misfortune for me alone."

Dusty screwed around, looked at Zytoff. The Black's face had become ashen white, but his deep-sunken eyes were like smouldering coals of fire. A wave of pity for the man swept through Dusty. But it vanished instantly as he thought of the thousands who had died a horrible death at AT-Twenty-two.

Face stony, he reached out for the gun, then crawled close to the Black. He put his weight on the other hand, leveled the gun at the Black's head.

"If they reach you in time, maybe you'll live," he said, forcing harshness into his voice. "Spill Fire-Eyes' plan of attack, or they'll never reach you alive.

"So help me, Zytoff—wounded or not, I'll let you have it right between the eyes if you don't talk. Why are the positions of the Tenth, Thirtieth and Forty-first squadrons so important? What is Fire-Eyes planning to do?"

Zytoff looked straight down the muzzle of the gun, and smiled.

"Not planning to do, my friend," he said through blood flecked lips. "Is doing, now—would be better."

"Doing what?" Dusty grated at him, eyes agate. "Let's have it, bum! See, I'm putting pressure on this trigger!"

A milky film spread over Zytoff's eyes. Then the eyelids fluttered closed. But the man's lips stayed back in a taunting smile, and he just managed to breathe out the words.

"One of your favorite expressions, my foolish friend—go to hell!"

Dusty stared at the limp body, slowly lowered his gun.

"Damn your hide!" he gritted. "But, you're half white, anyway!"

Zytoff's lips twitched, but no sound came from them, nor did his eyelids flutter open. Dusty stared at him a moment longer, realized that the man was still breathing feebly.

At that moment he heard somewhere in the distance the faint clanging of a bell gong. Instinctively he straightened up, gasped with pain but stayed upright. Then inch by inch, as fast as he could, he pushed himself up onto his feet.

He would have fallen over sidewise, but for a nearby table. Bracing himself against it, he swept his eyes about the room. Finally he found what he was looking for—the hidden door in the wall through which Zytoff had first entered.

"Come on, get going!" he grunted savagely at himself. "What the hell—waiting for them to serve tea, or something? Get the hell out of this place—and get out fast!"

Perhaps the self-lashing words had something to do with it. And, then again, perhaps they didn't. But at any rate, he shoved himself away from the table, and, like a man dead-drunk lurching from lamp post to lamp post, he went staggering across the room to the opposite wall. When he reached it he steadied himself for a second or two, then began fumbling about the crack outline of the door. But save for the quarter inch crack, his fingers slid over nothing but smooth wood. There was no knob or handle to the door, nor even a countersunk push-button.

Cursing softly, he went over every inch of the door and its connecting sides. Again he heard the distant clanging of the bell gong.

"Damn this thing!" he snarled and hurled himself against it.

And it happened! The door pivoted in the middle, and he went flying through into a cave of darkness!

CHAPTER 12
DUSTY TAKES OVER

UNABLE TO stop himself, he went rushing forward, feet hardly touching steel-plated flooring under him. Then, without warning, he crashed up against some invisible and immovable object, bounced back and sat down hard.

Instantly the darkness vanished, and the familiar parade of spinning stars and comets flooded his eyes with blinding light. He had the weird, eerie sensation that his head had been ripped from his shoulders and was floating off by itself through space.

Gradually, though, the stars and comets faded away before the onrush of returning darkness. And his head came back onto his shoulders again. He knew that for a fact. The piercing pain at the back of his neck had redoubled in intensity. Weakly, wobbly as a new-born kitten, he struggled up on his feet, and leaned against the object that had halted him so abruptly. It was a solid steel-girder-braced wall.

Twisting so that his back was against it, he relaxed for a moment to give his head a chance to stop spinning and renewed strength to flow back into his veins. It was then he saw why the door had opened so suddenly.

Through the crack on all four sides the light of the room which he had just left was filtering. In short, it was a swinging door, pivoted in the middle. Had he but pushed against it with his hand in the first place, instead of fiddling around for a disguised handle or a hidden release push-button, he would have opened it immediately!

"Numbskull!" he grated at himself. "You sure left your brains back on the drome!"

By now his eyes had become accustomed to the darkness, and he could see where he was. It was a four-foot wide companionway that led off in both directions. That is, to his right and to his left.

Squinting his eyes along it in one direction he saw nothing but the dim outline of bracing uprights and girders. And when he squinted in the opposite direction he saw exactly the same thing.

Closing his eyes, he tried to picture in his mind the relationship of his present position to the door he had been ushered through when he first met Fire-Eyes.

He had been walking aft then, and had gone left through the door. That would place this door, in front of him now, to the left of the main door to the room. That meant that this companionway, where he was now, ran crosswise through the ship. The port side was to his right, the starboard side to his left. In other words, he was somewhere on the water-line deck of the carrier, standing facing the stern.

"And so what?" he grunted thickly. "Dammit, I can't stand here for the rest of my life!"

It was at that moment he became conscious of something that had escaped him since the very moment he had come aboard. The carrier was in motion. In that other room, because of the thick rug probably, or the excitement of the occasion, he had not noticed the vibration.

But he could feel it now, and plenty—through the soles of

his boots, and in his back pressed against the girder-braced wall. And the moment he felt it he realized that the carrier was not loafing along at any cruising speed, either. Her electro-turbines were turning up maximum revs, and slamming the giant craft through the Atlantic at top speed.

"Navigating bridge and funnels on the port side," he murmured softly to himself. "Hum-m-m, so we'll head starboard until we get our bearings."

Pushing himself from the wall, he turned and started along the companionway leading toward the starboard side of the ship. Every step was like a step in bare feet on spear points. The slightest movement made his head light as a feather, and the rest of his body so much dead-weight lead.

The pain in the back of his neck became so intense that he was forced to bite down savagely on his lower lip to keep from groaning aloud. To ease the pain, if possible, he raised his left hand to his neck, felt sticky, blood-drenched raw flesh. It hurt him less when he left it alone.

A sudden dully clanking sound to his right brought him up short, his heart skipping every other beat. A soft shaky laugh spilled off his lips, as it came again, and he realized the cause.

The upright bracing girders projected out a bit into the companionway, and he had accidentally slapped his gun up against it. He had actually forgotten that the fingers of his right hand were still clutching the gun.

Shifting it to his left hand, he followed the wall with his right, and continued on his way. Presently the companionway stopped—that is, it split T-shaped. One section led aft, and the other toward the bow.

On sudden impulse he started toward the bow end—there was more light that way. But he had not rounded the corner, when he stopped short and ducked back into the cross-ships section.

Footsteps were coming along the companionway from the bow. Squeezing in behind the intersection upright girder, he slowly stuck his head out and peered around the corner.

For two or three seconds he could only hear footsteps. Then a pair of feet came into view. Then the flaring bottoms of sailor pants. Then a fatigue jacket. And lastly, the hawkish face of a Black seaman, with the close-fitting skullcap on his jet black hair.

Ducking back out of sight, Dusty grinned thinly. And for the first time in hours a thrilling warmth flooded through him. Here was exactly what the doctor ordered.

HOLDING HIS breath, gun raised and held poised, he waited still as death while the footsteps drew nearer and nearer. But when they were not more than a dozen yards from the corner upright girder behind which he crouched, they stopped dead.

Not daring to look, he waited in agonizing suspense. Thick-soled seaman's shoes shuffled on the steel deck; became silent and shuffled some more. Then they started hitting the deck again in firm steps—and the sound of those steps grew louder and louder in Dusty's strained ears. The Black was continuing his original course. The reason for his stopping would probably never be known. But, that didn't matter a damn.

Five steps away. Four steps—three—*one!*

A burly shadow crossed Dusty's line of vision. His eyes flew to the top part, the head, and just behind where the ear should be. And in perfect timing, as though his gun hand was synchronized with the retina of his eyes, he swung the gun down.

Dusty hit him right where he had planned—about three-quarters of an inch behind the seaman's left ear. The man slumped as if he had been hit by an anvil.

Rather than tax his strength by catching the man, Dusty let him hit the deck. Then, bending over, he caught hold of one of the seaman's hands and dragged him back into the cross-ships companionway. That accomplished, he placed his gun on the floor and began to strip off his own uniform.

Pain made sweat stream off his face, and his breath to come in quivering, rasping gasps. But somehow he managed it, and in due course he was garbed as a Black seaman.

Picking up the gun, he stuck it in the pocket of the fatigue jacket. On second thought, though, he jerked it out, took deliberate aim and smacked the muzzle down on the left temple of the sailor.

Pulling the man to the side, he jammed his limp figure back in the darker shadow cast by one of the projecting upright girders. Behind another girder he jammed the pilot's uniform he had taken off. Then, for a moment, he leaned against the companionway wall and fought to steady his jangling nerves.

Eventually, a matter of a couple of minutes, he succeeded in pulling himself together somewhat, rounded the corner and started down the companionway toward the bow.

He passed several doors leading off to unknown places, but he didn't pause. Up forward the bell gong was clanging at regular intervals. The sound came from the deck above. That would be the deck just under the flight deck.

The companionway made a sharp right angle turn to the right. He saw the companionway ladder about twenty feet ahead. Right hand sunk in the fatigue-jacket pocket, fingers curled comfortingly about the butt of the gun, he braced himself with his left hand and went up the companionway ladder.

It brought him out into a large dome shaped compartment. One snap glance around, and he knew what it was. The three trim Black Navy scouting planes to his right were sufficient. He was in one of the carrier's plane hangars.

There were doors on all four sides of the room. He selected the door on the bow end, moved quickly over to it. But as he reached his hand out for the knob, the door was suddenly swung away from him. Before he had time even to blink, a Black, with petty officer's insignia on his uniform, came through the opening. Both Yank and Black stopped dead, stared at each other. Dusty thought fast. He groaned aloud, swayed slightly on his feet.

"Have they found the American dog?" he gasped. "I was badly hit."

The petty officer gulped.

"You are injured!" he exclaimed. "Come, you must be taken to the sick bay."

Dusty shook his head.

"No, no!" he shouted. "I am better. But I have been unconscious since the shooting. Tell me what has happened?"

"There were two of them, as you probably know," came the reply. "One is now dead, with the great Zytoff, on the deck below. The Supreme One has left. I do not know if he was badly wounded or not. I saw blood on his tunic as he got into the plane. We are now searching the ship for the other dog. It will not be long."

"But the ship?" asked Dusty breathlessly. "It is going at top speed."

"But of course!" replied the petty officer, a faint puzzled frown creasing his brows. "The word has come—the American sea squadrons have changed their positions. There is nothing to stop us now!"

"The American squadrons?" echoed Dusty in forced jubilation. "You mean the Tenth, Thirtieth and Forty-first?"

The petty officer's frown deepened.

"What others but those?" he snapped. Then, harshly, "But how did you know their numbers. You—you have been eavesdropping, eh? When you were stationed behind the wall of that room to guard the Supreme One, you listened, eh?"

Dusty raised a protesting hand, shrank back as though fearing the wrath of this superior officer.

"But I have ears!" he said, putting a whine into his voice. "I could not help but hear—like the others. But the great Zytoff is dead, you say? It cannot be possible!"

"Have you no eyes?" rasped the petty officer, with just the faint trace of confused suspicion creeping into his voice. "Did

146

you not see that other American dog shoot him from behind the wall? Did you not see the blood spurt—see him fall over dead? Or were your ears your eyes?"

Dusty pointed at his bleeding neck and cheek.

"I saw very little before bullets from the dark struck me," he said. "I fell and knew no more."

The petty officer was frowning so deeply now that he almost looked crosseyed.

"That is very strange!" he muttered. "No one else was injured. I understood that the dog was behind the wall opposite to the one where the guard was stationed. Here, twist your face to the light. Let me have a good look at you!"

The petty officer's hand was on his gun. At that exact moment, however, the bell gong up forward started clanging furiously.

"The signal!" exclaimed the Black. "They have found the other dog! They—"

THAT WAS the last word that the petty officer spoke for a long time. At the sound of the bell he had half turned. He didn't have the chance to turn back. Dusty's gun laid open his face from ear to jaw bone. He emitted an eerie gurgling sound from his throat and folded up like a rickety deck chair. As he hit the deck Dusty already had him by the collar. One of the planes was about fifteen feet away. Dragging the petty officer like a sack of meal across the deck, he heaved him up, dumped him in the cockpit, and shoved the glass cowling shut.

"A little hangar flying for you, sweetheart!" he grinned.

Then pivoting, he slid through the open door and continued his way forward. Pain, and there was lots of it, was now practically forgotten. He knew definitely that Curly Brooks had saved his life; that he had nailed Zytoff, and maybe Fire-Eyes, too. Good old Curly, the one-man army, and how!

But Curly had been caught! Alive—or dead?

The torturing thought speeded up Dusty's footsteps. He practically ran down the companionway toward the ladder at the far end.

The bell was still clanging, and he knew now that it came from the port side of the flight deck. Just before he reached the ladder, he came to a companionway that led off toward the port side. Should he cross over that way, or go up the ladder and across the deck?

The few seconds he took to make up his mind were as a gift from the gods. He heard loud talking down the companionway leading to the right! Voices, Black Invader voices, were arguing vehemently.

"Of a certainty I can! Did I not fly with the great Zytoff last night? I watched him operate the Telsa gun!"

"I grant you that, my comrade!" cut in a deeper voice. "But I assisted with the experiments in Europe. I understand the timing of the liquid gas shells. That is a delicate operation, I assure you. Let us compromise. The great Zytoff is gone. We must do our part without him.

"You fly the plane, my comrade, and I will operate the Telsa gun. Together we shall kill them by the thousands. We know what Zytoff planned to do—to isolate the territory completely from the north until our forces have strongly entrenched themselves."

"But I insist—"

"Come, my good comrade, we waste valuable time. Let us agree to my proposal. You must, as junior officer. Come, let us go see what the American dog looks like, before we depart!"

There were a few grumbling words that Dusty didn't catch. He didn't have time to concentrate on hearing them. A thin beam of light on the companion way deck widened, just as he stepped back out of sight.

He heard the bump of a doorknob against the wall, and the shuffle of footsteps going away from him. Sticking his head around the corner, he saw two broad shouldered figures in black, walking rapidly toward the port side of the carrier.

He waited until they were practically out of sight around a slight bend. Then he spun around the corner and went forward swiftly and silently, yet on the alert to check his pace and go into action if the unexpected suddenly happened. But it didn't. That is, not until he had rounded the bend himself and was moving toward a narrow ramp that rose up to a level with the main flight deck.

As a matter of fact, it happened so quickly, his brain registered it about a quarter of a second too late. There came loud shouting from the top of the ramp. Several figures garbed in the uniforms of Black Invaders appeared.

One of them was suddenly catapulted outward amid vile curses. The figure went flat on the ramp, bounced twice, slipped and slid down the rest of the way, and finally came to a stop almost at Dusty's feet.

Frozen, he glanced down at the limp form. The man wore

the uniform of a Black navy commander, with senior pilot's rating. It was a uniform exactly like the one worn by one of the Blacks who had met him when he first came aboard. But as Dusty glanced at the face, his heart seemed to explode in his chest.

Regardless of the copper-tinted skin, the black bushy eyebrows, and jet shaggy hair, he knew that he was looking at the face of Curly Brooks!

CHAPTER 13
THE TELSA PLANE

FOR ONE infinitesimal part of a second, Dusty stood there staring down at his unconscious pal. Yet, even in that short time his brain raced over at top speed, grasped the utter hopelessness of the situation, and decided upon a wild plan of instantaneous action.

Screaming a mad curse in the Black tongue, he stooped over, grabbed hold of the slack of Curly's tunic and pulled him up on his feet. Holding him with one hand, he wildly brandished the other clenched fist.

"Dog of a dog!" he roared. "Your bullets would seek my life, would they? You would try to kill me as I trapped you? Now, you have been trapped, and a thousand deaths will be yours!"

Cutting himself off short, Dusty whirled toward the group of Black officers, who had halted halfway down the ramp. He singled out the senior officer, saluted with his free hand.

"For my injuries!" he roared at the Black, "let mine be the

first bullet to enter his heart. Tell me, my commander, where shall I take the dog?"

The senior officer advanced down the ramp a couple of steps.

"He is not to die yet," he said. "We will first get words from his lips—words that may help us. Take the dog to my quarters, and you shall have your revenge, later."

Dusty's heart started beating again. He wanted to sob aloud with joy. In the few seconds allowed he had discovered that Curly was not badly injured.

Brooks must have been taken unawares and slammed over the head with a gun or some other blunt instrument. There was a small gash about an inch up from the tip of the left ear. Curly was out cold, but he was breathing without difficulty.

"At your orders, my officer," said Dusty, and although the exertion made his head swim horribly, he heaved Brooks up on his shoulder and waited for the senior Black officer to stalk by him and on down the companionway.

Others followed, but with quick movements, Dusty slipped into step right in back of the senior officer. His heart was pounding so hard that he almost believed that it would drive his ribs out through his chest.

Part of the pounding was the result of the dead weight on his shoulder—it didn't help his pain-screaming body at all. And part of the pounding was exultant relief that his spur-of-the-moment plan had worked.

To have opened fire on that gang on the ramp would have brought death swiftly and surely to Curly and himself. Oh, he would have nailed a few of them, but the gunfire would have brought the entire ship's personnel on the run. And the automatic in his fatigue-jacket pocket would not have lasted long against the thousand-odd Blacks who made up the carrier's crew of officers and seamen.

Forward—left, right, left, right! Pain, pain, pain—shooting, with hot-pains in every cubic inch of his flesh and bones! Where in God's name were this rat's quarters? Were they at the end of the world?

In a dulled sort of way, he realized that they had turned off into another companionway. Maybe it was one through which he had come; maybe, it wasn't. He didn't know, and cared less just so long as they reached the damn Black's quarters before his strength gave out completely.

And then, as though coming out of a dream, he found himself staring through an opened door into neat but comfortable shipboard quarters. The senior Black officer was inside, and motioning for him to enter. He stepped over the raised, polished brass threshold and over to a chair the Black pointed at.

Gingerly, yet not so as to arouse suspicions, he deposited Curly in the chair, then hung onto the back of the chair himself, and sucked in his breath. At the same time he slid his right hand up toward his fatigue-jacket pocket.

But suddenly he cut short the movement, and let his hand fall back. On a small cabin shelf, not a foot from his head, was a Black Invader gas gun holster. And there was a gas gun in the holster!

Still holding one hand on the chair, he moved around in back of it so that his right hand was within grabbing distance of the holstered gas gun. But he didn't reach for it at once. Pretending a coughing spell, he bent over slightly, raised his free hand to his lips—which brought it within inches of the gas gun—and shot a furtive glance about the cabin from under his furrowed brows.

Within the next few seconds the whole situation would come to a head. If the senior officer ordered him out of the cabin, he was sunk. There'd be a fight, and that would be the end for him and Curly. Also, if that mob outside piled into the cabin, the result would be just as disastrous.

Not one of the damn rats was going to so much as lay a hand on Curly. No, not by a damn sight. It would be death all around, of course. But by God, the Blacks would know that they'd been in a fight when they woke up in hell.

The snarling voice of the senior officer cut off the rest of Dusty's thoughts.

"You, comrade seaman!" he barked, "do what you can to bring this dog back to where he can talk. There is brandy, there, on that shelf.

"Comrade lieutenant-commander, you will remain. You other comrades—back to your stations, and prepare for flight action immediately!"

IT WAS a crazy, cockeyed thought, but Dusty felt that he could almost kiss the Black for his words. Just two of them were going to remain! The others were being sent away.

Steeling himself, to stop his hands from shaking, Dusty turned and took down the bottle of brandy from the shelf. As he did, his eyes glanced through the single porthole in the cabin.

It looked out and down onto the main flight deck. Because of the peculiar angle at which the superstructure of the craft had been set on the port side, it was as though he were not on the carrier at all, but looking down at it from another ship.

That, however, was but a fleeting impression. Something else, a million times more important, met his gaze and held it transfixed. On the center of the main flight deck, not more than forty to fifty feet from where he stood, was a giant plane.

It was of the bi-plane type, and powered by four engines. The engines were in pairs, back to back, and placed between the wings halfway out from the cabin fuselage. Their mountings were perfectly faired, and save for the pointed snout fore and aft, they almost looked like solid mid-wing struts.

The cabin fuselage was of the conventional type, save for one most important detail. Located on top of the fuselage, in the nose was a round, flat-topped dome.

The muzzle of a five- or seven-inch gun projected out through a sealed opening.

Halfway out from the point where the gun projected through the sealed opening, the muzzle was clamped to the top of the cabin by a streamlined metal mounting. Its presence indicated at once that the recoil of the gun was absorbed by mechanism inside the turret.

One flash glance at it was all Dusty could afford. But as he pulled the brandy bottle down off the shelf and tugged at the cork, two thoughts streaked through his brain.

One was memory of the strange craft he and Curly had seen high in the air over AT-Twenty-two area; the other was memory of the conversation he had overheard not more than ten minutes ago. The Telsa gun! The Telsa gun that fired liquid-gas shells!

That craft out there was the answer to Atlanta and Roanoke! That craft out there was Zytoff's secret! The Telsa gun—liquid gas shells that created a diving whirlpool of yellowish-red flame and destroyed all it touched. Yes, wiped objects from the face of the earth, the surface of water, and out of the air!

"Steady with your hands, fool! Would you pour it on the rug instead of into a glass!"

The snarling words jerked Dusty back to the present. The senior Black officer, and the one whom he had addressed as comrade lieutenant - commander were watching him through angry eyes. In the nick of time he held the bottle upright before its contents splashed down onto the thick rug.

Mumbling humble apologies, he took a glass from the shelf, and poured some of the amber liquid into it. Putting the bottle back, he started to force the lip of the glass between Curly's lips, but the senior Black officer snatched it away from him.

"You spill too much!" he barked. "I will do this!"

Dusty nodded briefly. It gave him the one opportunity he desired. That is, it focused the entire attention of the two Blacks upon Curly Brooks. Stepping back until he was pressing against the cabin shelf, Dusty watched the two Blacks like a hawk.

The senior officer had grabbed Curly by the hair, forced his head back, and was jamming the glass between the unconscious Yank's lips. The other was pressing his thumbs cruelly against Curly's jaw bone to make him unclench his teeth.

Twisting slightly to hide his right hand, Dusty reached up

and snaked the gas gun from out of its holster. It felt awkward and clumsy in his numbed fingers. At that moment panic gripped him. The lieutenant commander was turning his head toward him. Yet for the life of him he couldn't swing up the gas gun and squeeze the butt clamp trigger.

One, two, three seconds of torturing hell dragged past. Through a roaring haze Dusty saw both Blacks jerk their heads around toward him. The glass slid from the hands of the senior officer, spilled brandy down the front of Curly's tunic, and fell noiselessly onto the rug. Stark hatred flared up in both Blacks' eyes, and like two mechanical dolls they went back a pace, opened their mouths.

The gun was up! Dusty squeezed hard. There was a faint hiss, and a thin stream of purple smoke spurted out from the tapered muzzle of the gas gun.

It caught the lieutenant-commander right square in the face. Even as he crumpled to the floor, Dusty swung the gun and blasted the deadly purple stream straight into the face of the senior Black officer.

IT ALL happened in the fraction of a second. But even as Dusty released pressure on the butt clamp he flung his other arm around Curly and pulled the lean pilot, chair and all back into the far corner of the cabin.

From past experience he knew that the deadly purple gas from a Black Invader gas gun lost its effect in the matter of split seconds. But he wasn't taking any chances. Holding his own breath, he pinched Curly's nose and clamped his other hand over the unconscious man's mouth.

His burning lungs were about ready to burst, and Curly's body was trembling slightly before he let out his own breath and took his hands away from Curly's face. Then slowly he relaxed, stared at the two motionless Black officers on the rug.

"At least you saw it coming!" he grated softly to himself. "And that's something!"

Half spinning, he darted over to the door through which he had entered, and softly slid a locking bolt into place. To his left there was another door. It was partly opened and led into a small stateroom. He stepped over to it, stuck his head inside, and saw a third door.

It opened onto a small gangway ladder leading down to the level of the main flight deck. A crooked grin twisting his lips, he slid its locking bolt home. Then he ducked back into the first room.

Curly was slowly rolling his head from side to side, and groaning faintly. Scooping up the brandy bottle Dusty spilled a bit of the liquid between Curly's lips. Brooks made a face, gagged and coughed slightly.

Then slowly his eyelids fluttered up. Glazed eyeballs became fixed on Dusty's face. Brooks blinked several times. Then a look of grim defiance seeped into his eyes. A violent tremor ran through his body, and his lips parted.

"Better go for your gun, rat!" he snarled.

"Silence, dog!" Dusty roared in the Black Invader tongue.

Then he leaned close to Curly.

"Take a good look, kid!" he whispered. "But pipe down! How do you feel?"

"You!" Curly gasped in a low whisper. "God, I thought they'd killed you—couldn't see you but I knew you were in that room. Say—they did get you! Your face and neck! You—"

"Never mind my face and neck, now!" Dusty cut in quickly. "Are you all right? Can you move? We've got to get out of here, pronto!"

"I'll be okay in a minute," came the faint answer. "Got clouted on the dome. I—I remember now. Dusty! There's a queer looking ship on the flying deck. Like the one we saw at AT-Twenty-two. I was taking a look at it. But a greaseball came out of the cabin, and I lost my head. I swung on him, and that's all I remember."

Curly Brooks stopped short as his eyes fell on the two Blacks on the floor. He pointed at them, looked at Dusty.

"Dead," Dusty nodded. "But listen, how the hell did you get to that room where he was—Fire-Eyes, I mean? And this uniform you've got on?"

Some color flooded back into Curly's tinted skin and he grinned.

"I had a hunch things were going haywire when they separated us," he said. "So when that mug was ushering me down a dark companionway, I slugged him. Swiped his uniform and shoved him into some kind of a closet, and locked the door.

"Then I went back in the direction you'd gone. Guess I got lost, 'cause when I went through a door I saw half a dozen Blacks peeking through slots in a wall. They all had guns to those slots.

"It was too late to turn back. A couple of them had seen me. I gave 'em a tough look, and walked past them. It was a sort of

.. A THIN STREAM OF PURPLE SMOKE SPURTED OUT.

between-the-walls passage that went around almost three sides of the room. Found a dark place that had a slot in it.

"I got there just as Zytoff started speaking English to you. Meant to get them both and rush in for you. But, the other rats started blazing away. Guess I went sort of coo-coo.

"When I saw you falling I planted some in Zytoff. Then I slapped a couple at Fire-Eyes. Think I hit him. Then hell broke loose. I ducked out meaning to come back as soon as I could. Got lost again. Saw that plane—and the lights went out."

"Wait, hold your horses!" Dusty finally shut him off. "Try to get up, kid. I've got ideas. I want you to put on this big shot Black's uniform. It's our only chance. That crate is just outside.

"I think it'll be taking off in a few minutes. We can get to it through a door in the next room. This is the ship commander's quarters. I haven't been spotted—tell you about it later. With you dressed as him we can make it. We—"

Dusty cut himself off short as the thought came to him. He leaned over, placed his hand on Curly's arm.

"Kid!" he whispered breathlessly. "You were with the Forty-first carrier squadron a week or so ago. Where were they stationed then? Or were they on just a routine patrol?"

Curly screwed up his face in deep thought.

"The Forty-first?" he echoed dully. "Oh yes, I was attached to the *Stamford*. She's the flagship. Why they went down to join the Tenth and Thirtieth super-cruiser and carrier squadron in the Florida and Bahama Islands patrol. The Forty-first replaced the Eighth and Sixteenth. They were transferred to Pacific coast duty. Why? What about them?"

160

Dusty stood stock-still for a couple of seconds. Then suddenly, he smashed his bleeding right hand into the palm of his left, and in his wild excitement didn't even feel the pain that shot up his arm.

"By God!" he breathed fiercely. "Of course—of course! Hurry Curly! For God's sake step on it! We've got to leave here, and now!"

Curly was pulling the carrier commander's uniform over the one he already wore.

"What's up!" he hissed.

Dusty helped him button up the tunic.

"The plan!" he whispered excitedly. "Fire-Eyes' plan! I've got it at last. God, we've been lunk-heads—figuring a Central Atlantic states attack by sea and air. Oh my God, the devils have pulled everything up there! Wiped out Atlanta and Roanoke—leaving it helpless."

"Leaving what helpless!" grated Curly. "For God's sake, what are you driving at?"

Dusty pulled him through the door into the small stateroom.

"The Blacks plan to nail Florida!" he hissed. "The one thing they've been waiting for was the Tenth, Thirtieth and Forty-first to be pulled up north. That's been done, now. I'm sure of it. It's a gigantic sea and air attack against Florida. Come on we've got to get a warning back to shore!"

CHAPTER 14
HELL'S FINALE

WITHOUT GIVING Curly a chance to make any comment, Dusty pulled him over to the door that led out to the short flight deck ladder. Sliding back the bolt he swung it open a couple of inches and peered out.

The giant biplane was still in the same place, in the center of the flight deck. Its nose was pointed toward the bow, which, as Dusty stuck his head out farther and saw, was empty of planes.

At the extreme cut-off point of the bow a small group of carrier greaseballs were lounging about.

Toward the stern a whole swarm of greaseballs and ordinary sailors were wheeling planes off the elevator platforms and rolling them into formation behind other planes already in position.

But no one was near the giant biplane, however. At least, not as far as Dusty could see. The cabin door was on the side facing him, and it was partly open. But though he peered hard toward the glassed-over cockpit in the tail section, he could see no movement to indicate pilots or greaseballs were inside.

Pulling his head back in again, he twisted toward Curly, jerked a thumb over his shoulder at the plane.

"We make a dive for it, kid," he said in a flat tone. "With that crate, I hope we can do plenty. But we take it off their hands, anyway. Okay?"

"Listens swell," was the quiet answer. "I wouldn't mind a

162

whirl at the controls of that baby. That damn gun thing looks interesting, too!"

"Save it!" Dusty snapped him down. "We go down, just as though we owned the boat, see? You a couple of steps ahead, because of your rank. I've still got a gun in my pocket. Walk fast, but not too fast.

"But when we get within jumping distance—jump fast. If I know my engines the ones on that crate are the preheated type—so they should click off the bat. All set?"

"I'm on my way," grunted Curly.

With that, Brooks pushed past him and started down the deck ladder. Dusty waited until he was at the bottom step, then went down himself. Contact with the flight deck sent millions of sharp tingles shooting through him. Not that the deck was electrified, but because only some thirty feet lay between Curly and himself, and the latest Black Invader weapon of the air.

Thirty feet! Yet in the next moment it seemed like thirty miles. Every part of him shouted for speed—shouted for him to race madly across the metal deck to the biplane. It took every ounce of his will power to hold himself in check; to walk a couple of paces to the rear of Curly, just as a Black sailor following his commander should.

But with each step he kept shooting his eyes toward the stern of the ship. Those forward didn't bother him at all. If they were going to have company, said company would come from the stern of the carrier. Back where fighting planes and scouting craft were being wheeled into place for a mass take-off.

And when they were but a short dozen steps from the half

opened door of the cabin, a voice called out in Black Invader lingo.

"My comrade commander! One minute, please!"

From the stern of the carrier running footsteps pounded along the deck. Dusty shot his eyes in that direction, and swore under his breath. The naval officer who had escorted him to the quarters of Fire-Eyes was running toward them.

"Keep on going, kid!" he hissed. "Go right on inside! I'll take care of him!"

Curly gave no sign that he had heard, but kept right on toward the ship, however. Walked right up to it, and pulled the door open wide, and started to climb in. Dusty quickened his pace slightly, so that he was right at Curly's heels.

By now, the naval officer was only ten yards away, and shouting at the top of his voice.

"My comrade commander! Do you wish a pilot for that plane? Do you intend to fly in it?"

The Black was at the cabin door now. He ignored Dusty, in his sailor's garb, and started to climb inside. It was his own tough luck for ignoring Dusty. He might have known what hit him, had he paid any attention. But he hadn't and he hit the deck so hard that he actually bounced.

Gun still clutched in his hand, Dusty leaped over the body and dived in through the cabin door. The instant he stopped, he whirled around and banged the door shut. For a split second, darkness blurred his vision.

Then he saw Curly hurling himself into the nearest seat.

Brooks' savage curse echoed back to Dusty—and his grated words.

"Where the hell's the engine starter pedal? Ah—there!" THE LAST word was drowned out by the whirring noise of spinning electric gears. A couple of seconds later, all four engines roared into life with a sound akin to a battle cruiser salvo.

Dusty rushed forward, and flung himself into the seat beside Curly. Brooks had released the wheel brakes, and the giant craft was rolling along the deck, picking up speed with every rev of its four propellers.

Like ants pouring out of their hill nest, Blacks poured out onto the deck of the carrier. Instantly the savage yammer and crackle of machine-gun and rifle fire came to Dusty's ears above the roar of the engines.

There was nothing for them to do but sit and take it—and pray for the best.

The cut-off bow of the carrier swept toward them at express train speed. Dusty held his breath, and waited. On they thundered, right up to the very lip of the bow. Then Curly pulled back on the controls.

Two, three seconds of hellish sinking sensation, and finally, as though reluctant to leave the carrier deck, the big plane lumbered slowly up into the air.

Once clear, though, it picked up speed and climbed steadily upward. Dusty didn't bother to look back. He knew that Black pursuits would be racing off the carrier and up after them. But they had to risk that for awhile.

"Keep climbing, Curly!" he yelled. "But zigzag a bit! They'll

be letting loose with their anti-aircraft guns in a moment! I'm
going to—"

As though his words had been a signal to the Black gunners,
five puffs of sooty smoke dotted the sky in front of them—one
after the other in rapid succession. Almost at the same instant,
Dusty heard a dull thumping sound on the cabin roof. He didn't
bother to look up, but he knew that high speed anti-aircraft
shrapnel had smacked them.

Shooting out both hands, he clamped radio ear-phones over
his head with one hand; snapped on radio contact, spun the
dial knob to the official H.Q. reading, and grabbed up the
transmitter tube with the other.

"Attention, Washington!" he roared into it. "Florida area in
danger of immediate enemy attack. Speed all possible help there
at once. Believe enemy will make attack against both east and
west coasts. A combined sea and air attack. A-Six speaking!
Relay attack alarm at once. Florida area in danger! Florida area
in danger! S.O.S. Emergency!"

The signal light on the radio panel blinked rapidly, but he
didn't bother to tune into the signals. He knew that it was a
request from Washington H.Q. for a check-back. They undoubtedly wanted more details. He didn't have them. He knew
only the main item regarding the attack. And so, ignoring the
blinking light, he shouted his S.O.S. call over and over again.

The plane was now at high altitude, and Curly was maneu-
vering it this way and that, so as to keep clear of the blazing
bursts from the high angle anti-aircraft guns aboard the Black
carrier.

"They're overtaking us, Dusty!" Curly shouted aloud, suddenly. "And there are no damn machine guns on this crate! I don't see any!"

Dusty repeated his S.O.S. call once more, then jumped up. There was a ladder in the nose of the ship. He rushed toward it, ran up the steel rungs. As he guessed, the ladder led to a small circular platform.

Standing on the platform his head and shoulders projected up into the round turret. On a panel in front of him was a mass of instruments. A flash glance at them told him that they were instruments for shell explosion timing, range finding, angle of fire, and so forth. At the bottom of the panel there was a small lever, fitted with a spring grip.

About two feet above his head was the rear end of the six-inch gun that stuck out through the sealed opening at the front of the turret. On both sides of the barrel of the gun, where it projected out through the turret, there was a small oblong glass port that permitted him to look out at the skies directly ahead.

The rear of the gun was about three times the size of the loading breach of the ordinary six-inch gun. It looked like five cylinders fitted together to form a solid circle. The front end tapered down into the main part of the gun barrel.

From the rear end of the cylinder at the bottom there was a seven-inch U-shaped loading tray leading back to a circular honeycomb arrangement at the rear of the turret. And in each of the cells of the honeycomb there was a brass nosed shell.

As Dusty stared at the whole thing, his heart sank. He knew

that it was a rapid fire type of gun, but how the hell it worked was beyond him.

Suddenly, though, he let out a wild shout of joy as the truth came to him. He realized that the multiple cylinder shaped breach revolved just as does the loading chambers of an ordinary revolver. He also noticed the small lever at the bottom of the honeycombed shell caisson, and realized its use instantly.

Reaching out, he pulled it down. There was a slight whirring noise. The caisson revolved until one of the cells was in a direct line with the loading tray. A split second later, the shell was pushed out by a bumper rod against its base. Down the tray the shell slid, and its driving band tripped a small trigger arm that projected up through the bottom of the loading tray, about six inches from the rear end of the bottom cylinder of the loading breach. There was a sharp snapping sound, and the rear end of the cylinder twisted outward and swung back clear of the loading tray.

The movement was perfectly timed, and the bumper rod pushed the shell into the cylinder. Then the bumper rod traveled backward, dragging along the bottom of the loading tray, and tripped the trigger arm in the reverse direction.

Instantly the rear end of the cylinder swung back, and slowly screwed itself into place. And tiny recoil locking lugs dropped down into their grooves. Back went the bumper rod and disappeared inside the honeycomb cell.

Dusty still held the lever down. There came the whirring noise again, and the shell caisson revolved until another shell was in line with the loading tray. And the loading operation was repeated all over again. The only difference being that as the driving band tripped the trigger arm, the multiple cylinder breach of the gun moved around one cylinder.

Heart thumping madly, Dusty held the lever down until all five cylinders in the breach had been loaded. Then he released the lever and peered hard at the dial panel. In the very center there were five dials all in a row, and they were numbered from one to five. The dial was graduated in seconds and minutes (Black Invader figures, of course). And printed in the center of each dial were the words

EXPLOSION TIMING

Reaching out, Dusty turned the knob of each dial until all needles pointed to the same figure. Then he glanced at the other dials. One was for range, another for angle of fire, and a third for speed of fire.

At that moment the fury of hell itself blasted against the outside of the turret.

"Dusty! For God's sake, we've got to do something! The sky is full of the rats!" Curly's voice came over the loudspeaker connected with the control room.

Dusty didn't take time to answer. Through the glass ports on either side of the gun barrel, he could see the two squadrons of Black planes thundering toward them. Other Black ships were even closer. Tearing his eyes from the sight, he reached over to the instrument panel, and set the dials to the best of his ability. Then twisting his head down toward the ladder opening, he shouted into the mouthpiece.

"Curly! Straighten her out on a level course, and hold her there. I'm going to take a chance on using this damn gun!"

As Curly's acknowledging shout came back to him he was already gripping the small lever fitted with the spring grip.

"Here goes!" he roared, and squeezed hard.

Swi-s-s-h!

A jolt like an electric shock streaked up his arm, and a blast of hot air smacked against his cheek. He let out a yelp and staggered back. But as his eyes looked through the ports he saw a ball of yellowish-red appear in the air, just in front of the on-rushing planes. One of them actually plowed into it, and seemed virtually to melt apart in thin air. A second later the ball of yellowish red flame flickered and faded out.

It was then that Dusty realized that he'd released his grip on the spring handled lever. He grabbed the lever again and squeezed it tight. *Swis-s-s-h! Swis-s-s-h! Swis-s-s-h! Swis-s-s-h!* Four times in rapid succession, and a terrific blast of hot air rushed through the round shaped turret. But Dusty was prepared this time and he had braced himself.

Seconds later the sky just over the advancing planes became marked by a wavy circle of sparkling yellowish-red. It swooped down over the Black ships, and in a terrific flash of light blasted them out of the sky. Four or five seconds later the ring of fire grew weaker and weaker, until finally it faded out into nothing.

"Got it! Got it this time!"

SHOUTING THE words at the top of his voice, Dusty spun toward the loading lever under the honeycomb caisson, pushed it down and held it there until all five cylinders of the breach had been reloaded.

It was during the second loading that he got the answer to a question that had come to his mind. That was, how the empty shell casings were ejected. He knew how, now. There was an oblong chute leading downward from a point just under the bottom breach cylinder. And there was an oblong flap running the entire length of each cylinder.

In short, when a shell was fired, and the cylinder holding the empty shell had revolved around to the chute, the flap was automatically opened. Thus the shell dropped down into the chute, and the flap was swung shut before a new shell was shoved into the cylinder.

A split second to realize that, and Dusty was squinting out through the ports at the sky filled with Black ships. They were trying to close in from the side—obviously keeping clear of the death trap area. Streaking out his free hand Dusty readjusted the dials.

"Bank left, Curly!" he bellowed into the mouthpiece. "Slam right at them. I've got the hang of this, now!"

Instant movement of the craft told him that Curly had heard, and was obeying orders. Through the glass port he saw four solid squadrons of Black planes start to break up formation and swing off into the clear. He laughed harshly and reached for the spring-handled lever.

"Yeah?" he grated. "Like hell you do! Have some of your own medicine!"

With that he squeezed the spring grip and held it squeezed.

The swishing sound echoed around in the gun turret, and hot air almost blasted him off his feet. Through blurred eyes he suddenly noticed a chain metal helmet hanging on the turret wall to his right. But it was too late to try to put on the thing, now.

The heavens outside had now become a sea of raging flame. Raging flame in the form of a gigantic circle that swooped downward through the Black planes. Like flies caught in a blast furnace they literally shriveled up one after the other.

Then and then only, Dusty released his grip, turned and reached a third time for the caisson loading handle. But no sooner had he reloaded the Telsa gun than he heard Curly's voice come roaring through the transmitter.

"Dusty—Dusty! For God's sake, look ahead to the left—that plane swinging south!"

Dusty snapped his eyes toward the port hole, stared across the air space. His heart looped over in his chest, and he let out a choking gasp. A giant cabin plane was racing southward, its pilot obviously striving frantically to get clear of the deadly liquid gas shells. But it was not the design of the plane, or its movements, that started Dusty's blood surging through his body. It was the insignia on the fuselage. There was the conventional Black Invader flag, but beside it was painted a green mask with only eye slits showing.

"Fire-Eyes!"

There was no time to make an accurate calculation of the range. He grabbed hold of the firing lever.

"Curly! Swing straight toward it—give the engines every damn thing they will take!"

"Swinging now!" came through the transmitter.

Eyes glued to the plane ahead, Dusty waited until it was tail section on to him, then he pulled the lever down and squeezed with every ounce of his strength. Once again the turret echoed with hissing, swishing sound, and hot air blasted against him, seemed to sear every square inch of skin on his face. But he steeled himself and held the firing lever down until the Telsa gun was empty.

Releasing the lever, he spun around, virtually fell down the ladder, and rejoined Curly. Neither of them spoke. Like two stone statues they sat rigid, eyes clamped on the heavens ahead.

THE GIANT cabin plane was swerving this way and that, as its pilot tried frantically to race out from underneath a gigantic, hovering ring of flaming yellow and red. For one split second the pilot almost succeeded. But at that very instant, as though the Devil himself had been waiting, the horrible ringed death swooped down and completely enveloped the banking plane. Instantly a fountain of fire belched upward, and something went flying off into space—flying off entirely clear of the ring of flame.

Mechanically, Dusty's eyes followed it.

"Curly—look there—my God—see who it is! Fire-Eyes, Curly! Fire-Eyes—he was blown clear of the plane!"

The rest stuck in Dusty's throat.

Clearly he saw the coarse black uniform, the big gauntlets, and the green mask, and skull cap. Fire-Eyes—Fire-Eyes hurtling down to a hell all his own. Wind caught the massive figure, flung it this way and that. Spun it over and over. It smashed into the rolling waters of the Atlantic, and disappeared from view. White foam marked the spot for a few seconds, and then even the foam disappeared. The waves continued rolling eternally onward.

"Got him—good God, Dusty—he's gone—forever!"

Curly's words came to Dusty as an awed whisper. He turned to his pal, tried to say something, but the words just wouldn't come from out of his throat. From head to foot he felt like so much jelly held together by the uniform he wore. Fire-Eyes—gone forever? The curse of the civilized world removed for all time? It didn't seem possible!

"Damn! Dusty, lend a hand, here! Something's gone screwy with the controls. I can't hold her up! She's—she's going out of control! Hold fast!"

Long before Curly had finished, Dusty knew that the Telsa plane was slip-sliding helplessly downward through the air. He tugged savagely with Curly on the controls, and got the nose up a bit. That didn't help much. They had lost too much altitude. The uninviting waters of the Atlantic, the rolling graveyard of Fire-Eyes, were directly below them.

But as he snapped his eyes to the left, beyond where the Black commander had gone to his doom, he saw smudgy smoke low down close to the water. He knew what was under that smoke—high speed destroyers of the Black Navy.

He suddenly caught Curly's eye, read the same thought in them. He grinned tightly.

"Not our day either, kid, I guess," he said with a shaky laugh. "Oh well—I guess the gang won't have much trouble finishing it up, now. Nice to have known you, kid."

"Yeah, it has been nice," said Curly in a husky voice. "And—anyway, we're going together. Always hoped it would be this way—if it had to happen."

There was no time for either of them to say anything else. Like a tired bird, completely exhausted from a long flight, the big plane staggered down and hit the water sidewise. Darkness, and utter silence caved in on top of him.

WHEN DUSTY opened his eyes again, he had the feeling that he'd just awakened from a bad dream. He tried to move, but a million pains shot through him, and he went limp with a groan.

"It's true, kid, we're still alive!"

Dusty managed to turn his head in the direction of the voice. It was then that he realized where he was—under the sheets of a hospital cot. Some four feet from him was another cot. And propped up in that cot, head and one arm swathed in bandages was Curly Brooks. Beyond Curly stood three motionless figures. They were General Horner, Biff Bolton, and Agent 10. Dusty blinked stupidly. Then memory suddenly rushed back.

"Then—then—" he began and stopped.

"Right!" came Curly's low voice. "They weren't Black Navy ships—one of our own destroyer flotillas. And they confirmed what we saw—Fire-Eyes taking the permanent water cure, I mean."

Dusty slowly raised his eyes and looked at General Horner. There was an expression on the Intelligence chief's face that he had never seen before. The big man looked like a father who has just been told by the doctor that his sick son has passed the crisis, and will live. He nodded jerkily.

"That is right, Ayres," he said in a choked voice. "We know definitely that he has gone for good. Who he was, God only knows—and I hope we never find out."

"Say!" Dusty suddenly asked. "The attack on Florida?"

"A complete failure, thank God!" was the reply. "They must have learned what you two had done. When they still had a chance of victory they retreated—raced off like rats. Yes, I guess it's over.

"Their devilish leader is gone. Their morale will break, now. We'll smash them out of Canada in a month. Shortly after that, their grip on Europe will be broken, too. Yes, son—it's about over. And I don't know what to say. I don't know how to—"

The man's voice failed. The hovering silence that comes after the roaring storm settled over the room. Those four men, who had done so much together, simply looked at each other through misting eyes. Hundreds of words were on each man's tongue. But in that moment no one could say a thing, for it was a moment in the lives of men when mere words would be utterly inadequate.

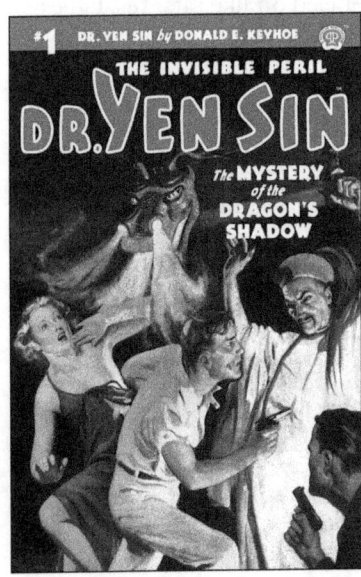
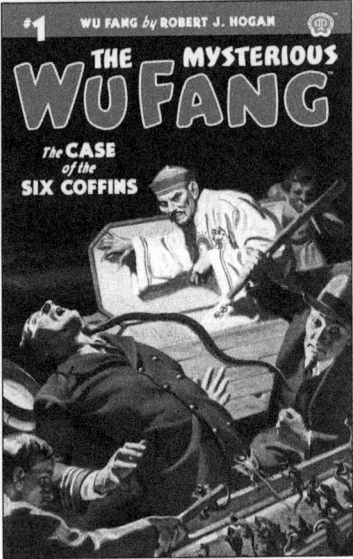

www.ingramcontent.com/pod-product-compliance
Lightning Source LLC
Chambersburg PA
CBHW061136200626
46817CB00016B/1665